The Killer

Watch Out

Megan Rose

Order this book online at www.trafford.com
or email orders@trafford.com

Most Trafford titles are also available at major online book retailers.

Printed in the United States of America.

ISBN: 978-1-4669-0815-4 (sc)
ISBN: 978-1-4669-0816-1 (hc)
ISBN: 978-1-4669-0817-8 (e)

Library of Congress Control Number: 2011962678

Trafford rev. 01/10/2012

 www.trafford.com

North America & international
toll-free: 1 888 232 4444 (USA & Canada)
phone: 250 383 6864 ♦ fax: 812 355 4082

Contents

First Step 1

Questions 4

School 7

Party Gone Bad 11

The Newspaper 16

The Search 18

Closer to the Truth 21

My Big Bro's visit 23

The Incident in the Bathroom 27

Carved 31

Alone 33

Hunting 35

On my Own 38

Journey to the Haunts Mansion 40

Arrived 42

Home at Last 45

The Mirror 47

Imagination 49

Secrets 52

The New Kid 58

Creepy 61

Bloody 63

I Don't Know You 66

Lies 69

Follow 72

What's next? 77

Revealed 79

Discussion 81

The Scary Dream 85

Gone 88

First Step

Every night, before I go to bed, I wonder how it must feel for those who are obligated to watch their loved ones die. The pain must be so dreadful. Then I wonder what if that happened to me? I mean I would loathe the thought of anyone attempting murder upon my family and friends. If you were to count up all the killings that happened in one day, your head would throb and break into millions of pieces. As astonishing as it sounds, most murderers slaughter because of jealousy and anger. I never thought that anyone could be neither jealous nor angry at me; until the whole charade began on a Sunday night.

It was a cold and windy night in Washington. The girl was twelve years old and her name was Melissa Cote. No one knew who the person that killed her was. That part remains unknown. "Melissa Cote was left by herself on Thursday night, and around 11:30pm there was a loud gun shot." The neighbor said across the street. We have the police checking out the place. One of the police men said, "I was walking up the stairs and went into the bedroom on the left side, as soon as I walked in I saw that there was blood splattered all over the dresser, bed, and walls. On the floor there were four bloody footprints that lead to the window. I went over to check it out and a hand grabbed my foot, it was a girl. She was lying up against the bed and was bleeding really heavy. Gruesome it was indeed." "This is reporter Dayne asking who has done this to an innocent girl? Is this person going to do it again? Well, we'll find out sooner or later."

I put down the newspaper and placed my coffee in the cup holder, staring in awe at every inch of the paper. I honestly couldn't believe that it was my cousin. I know this because they have a picture of her next to the article. My name is Vanessa Martinez and I'm 15 years old. Melissa was my favorite cousin; we used to do everything together. I feel bad for getting mad at her, because according to the article it was Thursday night and I wanted her to go to the movies with me. I wish I could say I'm sorry.

Apparently, I'm alone in my house because my parents had to go to a business meeting for a couple of months. Guess that means freedom for me. But was it so free after all?

I went up to my room to find something to do. I went over and picked up a book. I thought it might've been interesting by the cover. As I read the beginning, chills ran throughout me as if someone put the air conditioner on full blast, but I knew that couldn't be considering the air was off and it was very much in the middle of October as well. The novel had started off creepy; people were killing over people to get to this one person and it was just horrible. Tonight was still quite cold and windy out as it has been for the past few nights. There was a subtle noise coming from outside my door. It was intimidating. Should I dare go to the door? Maybe I should just stay put to be on the safe side. But, whatever it was, I could hear it breathing and I'm shivering vigorously.

These chills that ran throughout my body were nothing compared to this. Then, out of the blue, a palm sized piece of paper slipped under my door. I bent over to grab it and as I was picking it up, it said, "First step has been completed, next step is just around the corner." The note had made no sense to me. So many questions went through my head. Like, Who wrote this? Was there really someone at my door? What should I do? Maybe I'm just picturing this?" I laid down in my bed thinking about it; wondering of all the possibilities. I even wondered why the writing was so sloppy . . . The writing made me so suspicious because of the fact that it had seemed as if someone had just did it and ran off. I tossed and turned for hours. After a while, I remembered that I had school in the morning; I tried to dormant myself. Eventually, it worked, I fell asleep like a baby.

Questions

Ah, cherry Coca-Cola and cereal covered in chocolate milk is the way to go. My parents always told me when I was little that I had a passion for odd things; especially with what foods I eat and the time I eat them. A few years ago, If I do comprehend correctly, it was dinner time. Everyone was eating pork chops with a side of mashed potatoes and corn to go along with it. Meanwhile, I would grab me some freshly toasted toast, take out the peanut butter, take out the cream cheese, and I'd grab a knife and slap on the peanut butter and cream cheese onto both slices of the bread. Afterwards, I'd make my own fruity drink throwing any kind of fruit I could find and throw it into the blender. Yum, boy that was some good stuff.

While tapping my nails against the table creating a beat, a sound of a car beeping came from outside my house. I went over to the window with my soda and saw that it was for me. I walked outside and offered them some of it. Of course it was too early for them and besides it looked like they had more important things to talk about. "What happened yesterday?" My best friends Zack and Destiny asked as I got in the car for school.

Destiny is sixteen and has light brown hair with baby blue eyes. She's very attractive; a lot of guys at high school think she's hot and are always asking her out. She is also Latina, which is cool because I get to speak Spanish around her and Zack wouldn't even know what we're talking about.

Zack is very fun to be around. He has dirty brown hair and brown eyes. Most of the time he wears cologne. Sometimes it even smells good too. Zack says it'll impress the ladies and make them want him to be their man. I think that's crazy because it never really works, although he thinks it will. Plus, he doesn't wear yummy smelling cologne all the time. One time, he tried hitting on a girl and offered her to smell his cologne she nearly passed out. He thought it was the fact that she couldn't handle him; that surely wasn't the case.

"We tried to call you yesterday night, but at first we heard the dial tone and then nothing, nada. It was like someone cut the wire." said Destiny. "I wanted to come over but my mom wouldn't let me." Zack said.

I stared at them. I inhaled and exhaled continued by a question. "Didn't you guys hear about my cousin? She got killed. Other than that, something very weird happened yesterday. I felt like someone was near me right outside my door." Destiny was driving the car while putting on her glossy lip-gloss. Perfect way to get into an accident, huh? As Destiny rubbed her lips together spreading the gloss all over her lips, she asked, "Are you sure it wasn't your mom or dad? They were probably just checking up on you to see if you were sleeping and if not they gave you the clue that you should be sleeping or something." I gave her the 'Are you kidding me?' look. "No, Destiny it wasn't. I told you already that they were going away on a business meeting for a couple of months, do you not remember?" Destiny took a few moment to answer because she had to think if she remembered me telling her this. Finally, when we reached the third stop light, "Oh! Now I remember. I just had to take a few moments to think 'cause I do recall being distracted by one of my fingers being bigger than the other." At first my facial expression grew annoyed, but soon turned down to a chilled face. She tried showing me the difference between her two fingers, but I ruined her fun in that because if her hands weren't on the wheel in the next few seconds we'd be heading into a building.

"I got a note with blood stains on it . . ." Zack turned to pat my shoulder, held for a slight second, and brought it back down to his side. "Maybe you were picturing it? Like maybe seeing Melissa in the newspaper dead really shook you?" Destiny gave him a little shove. "Vanessa that's really scary. Do tell what that note said." I replied, "It said that the first step is complete and the next step is just around the corner; I had no idea what that could've meant."

School

The rest of the way, we sat there quietly; neither of us spoke one word to each other after my statement. I guess Zack and Destiny had to sink in what they have heard or maybe they were too busy glossing lips or putting on layers of cologne to choke someone to death. When we arrived at school, the first thing we saw was people lying on the ground. I tried to ask them why but no one responded. They only had scared looks on their faces. It was like they saw a ghost or something terrifying. We ended up walking passed them and entered the school. Destiny eventually spoke up and asked me in a scared and warily voice, "You know, this is weird." "Which part? The part with the creepy people lying on the ground or the part where they couldn't speak up?" I asked. "Both. Can you not see that ever since Melissa passed away, things have been hectic?" I rather not answer that particular question; I looked over at Zack to see if maybe he'd interrupt and take over the conversation. He didn't. The dude was too busy staring at his feet and trying his best to avoid anything we say. Destiny and I said bye to his lazy self-afterwards due to the fact that he had a different class he had to hustle to.

We went to our class to find that only five other students were there. What's this? Only five students? Where are the rest? Did something horrid happen to them? Or maybe they were just chicken to come to school because their afraid they'll get killed. Please. The place is filled with security guards. Tough ones too. No one would even make it pass them considering the fact that they have a taser.

I took a seat next to Germy Godzilla. His names actually Gregory Dickinson, but he is one big guy and likes to touch everything after he sneezes or coughs. Maybe he's the reason why most of the class is empty.

Our teacher, Mr. Spike, started talking about the digestive system. Something seemed wrong. Why wasn't he making jokes? Normally, he would think of something to say that was really funny and we'd all be dying on the floor from laughing too hard. He turned into some sort of zombie with no feelings. Also, Mr. Spike was my favorite teacher of all time until he decided to become boring. So, Mr. Spike continued talking about the digestive system, and how the food is processed after eating a meal, when someone came to the door. It was a tall, slim man. He was wearing black pants, a black and white striped shirt with a tie, and was carrying a brown suitcase. Also, he had dark brownish black eyes, and wore sunglasses on top of his head.

Mr. Spike told Germy Godzilla to hand out papers while he converses with the man. I overheard them talking about a code. "Here, Vanessa, take your paper." I gave him a disgusted look. "Thanks germy." He slammed down the papers. "One of these days someone's gonna get payback on you. They'll teach you what it's like to be hurt." Boy, this kid was actually smart. "I'm just telling you the truth." "yeah? Well get off my back Martinez. Just 'cause you get everything you want doesn't mean you can go around bullying people. Learn some manners." "It's not my fault I have loads of money from my parents being business people. Oh, and for your information I do have manners I said thanks didn't i?" I ignored him after that. I simply gave him a look and went back to drawing my attention on Mr. Spike and the man. I think I caught Mr. Spike tell the guy what the code was, so I wrote it down. 'A step closer to death, six, six, five.' Then the bell rang.

As If 1ˢᵗ period wasn't weird enough, 6ᵗʰ period was very peculiar. When I walked into class I saw Destiny and Zack and told them about the code. I know what you're thinking, why didn't I tell Destiny during first period? Well, there clearly wasn't enough time; I had to pick up all the papers that fell off my desk, and Destiny didn't wait for me. "Vanessa, why'd you right this down?" Destiny asked. "I don't know, I thought it would be useful in the future." Destiny had a slight panic in her voice as she said, "What if it's a scam? Or what if someone did that intentionally? Or what if_" Zack cut her off. "Would you relax? Why are you so tense for? And stop with the 'what if's'. There's no point in that. I'm sure it has nothing to do with Vanessa." Destiny began biting her nails. Then, I spoke up. "I don't know if I should worry or not. So for now let's not worry about it. Okay?"

The same man from 1ˢᵗ period walked in. "Hello class, I'm your new teacher from now on." Some guy in the back asked where Mrs. Barley was and the man replied, "She had to be taken care of." Then the guy smiled at Zack, Destiny, and I. I was very suspicious. Something wasn't right at all. Why? Of all people why him for a new teacher?

After class let out, we went to lunch. There was barely anybody in the cafeteria. Destiny started getting shaky and her face was turning pale. I was freaked out. "What's wrong?" I waited for a reply, but I didn't get anything from her. She sat there with her mouth wide open, struggling, with no words coming out.

Zack was bleeding on the back of his neck and I don't know why. "Are you ok?" I asked him in panic. "I-I don't know." Zack struggled with his words and when he said know, it faded away.

It was getting colder in the cafeteria and it just kept getting even colder and colder. I tried to move next to Destiny but I couldn't move at all. I kept on wondering what could possibly be going on. Then, something moved rapidly. I couldn't see what it was though. All of a sudden the thing was gone and so was Zack. The cafeteria went back to its normal self. It wasn't cold in there anymore. I looked at Destiny, she didn't look too pale anymore and I was able to move again. The frightened look was on both our faces.

Party Gone Bad

"Yo, Destiny?" We were sitting on the roof top of my house drinking lemonade. "Yes?" She replied. I shifted a little bit before saying what I needed to say. "Zack's gone. Something happened to him. He was there, and then he wasn't." Destiny, shocked, yelled and screamed because she was upset. "What! In the cafeteria? Are you sure he didn't just leave fast? How could this be!?" "I don't know. Maybe he's a magician." I said sarcastically. "But if he did leave how come he didn't call one of us?" "Well, I think he will! I don't wanna lose hope just yet!" I picked up my phone. "Alright, let's call him then." I dialed up his number and we waited for him to pick up. "Hello?" Destiny and I rolled our eyes. "Nice. Just real nice. We thought something devastating happened to you, you jerk." I said aggravated. "It was cold inside the cafeteria. So, I went to my locker to get a jacket, but when I came back no one was there. Then, I went home and waited for one of you to call me. I didn't bother calling because I knew one of you would have ended up getting in touch with me in the long run. "I see, I see." I replied in relief. Destiny then decided that she would jump right into the conversation. "Zack! I was freaking out! Is your neck ok?" Zack took a moment to answer. "It hurts like hell. The bleeding stopped eventually. And, you always freak out Destiny. Why is that?" Destiny got infuriated at Zack. "Well gee, sorry for caring!" I didn't have the time for another one of their mini fights. "Ok, Shut up, the both of you. It's nice that it's not bleeding Zack. It's Bad because it hurts. The great thing is, is that you're safe." "Yeah . . . hey look, I was on the phone with my girlfriend and she wanted me to invite you two to her 'Parents out of town. Let's get wild' party." Destiny and I exchanged looks. "Of course! When is her party?" "Tonight. I'll pick you girls up."

"Let me see your neck." I pulled his head towards me. Scratch marks were there. They were quite deep too. You could see the dry blood marks come across the whole neck scattered. It was definitely not a pretty sight to see. Destiny over-looked his neck too. "EW! That's some nasty scar!" Zack quickly covered his neck with one of his hands. "Thank you so much Destiny for pointing it out. How will I explain this one to my girl?" "You'll figure something out. You're an intelligent guy." I encouraged him.

We knocked on his girlfriend's door and waited for someone to answer the door. I found it funny how Zack, besides Destiny, is my best friend, and I never even knew his girlfriend's name nor even met her. I laughed at the thought as it lingered in my head.

"Zack!" They kissed. "Hey Babe, I'd like you to meet Destiny and Vanessa." She turned to Destiny first, "Hey, I heard you're the crazy, melodramatic girl." "Oh, really? That's my name card?" She crossed her arms glaring at Zack. Then, Zack's girlfriend turned to me. "And you, I heard that you get sarcastic a lot and you're a cranky bully sometimes." Oh wonderful. "Yep. That's me, I just love my label." I copied Destiny. I crossed my arms and said to Zack, "You better watch yourself buddy,

unless you might get jumped by Destiny and I one of these days."
Destiny and I both laughed. "Oh!" Zack's girlfriend said. "Silly me, feel
free to come in! Oh and by the way I'm Courtney." We walked into the
huge place and all I could see is a load of beer. "How old are you?" I
asked directing my finger in the direction of the beer. She came closer
to me and sort of whispered. "We're under aged, but that doesn't matter,
there's no way the cops will find out . . . unless you tell them?" I glared
at her. "Where's the bathroom?" Rolling her eyes she said, "Upstairs to
the left."

I left the loud noise and went to the bathroom. While I was in the
bathroom, someone knocked on the door. "Someone's in here!" Some
more knocking appeared. "I said, someone's In here!" After I said that,
the door knob jiggled. It was like someone was trying to open it. When
I finished I felt awkward. I noticed that Courtney left her safe opened.
I was intrigued to peek inside it. What a surprise I got. In it, the money
was gone. There must have been a break in while this Courtney chick
was out partying. Words were written across the safe in big blood red
paint. 'Get out now while you still have your life.' I had a chill run
throughout my body. I must warn the others.

I ran downstairs in panic. First, I went up to Destiny who was
sitting by herself on the couch. "We need to leave. Now." Destiny stared
at me. "Why?" it was hard for me to speak. I was too scared. Maybe I
do have something to worry about. "No time for explanation something
despicable will happen." "How do you know?" "Destiny! I said this is no
time for questions! We need to get everyone out of this place!" I shouted.
I ran over to Zack and his girlfriend. Maybe they'll listen to me better
than Destiny. Of course, I was wrong. "Zack, Can you stop making out
with Courtney and maybe listen to me for a sec?" Zack and Courtney
stared at me. I was talking to both of them now. "We need to get
everyone out of here. We are not safe. Something will happen soon and
I don't want to be here for it." They glared in disbelief. "Look Vanessa, I

know you always liked Zack so, of course you're going to try and make up something to get alone with him." I was so mad at her. My ears were flaring out smoke. Now I remember why I never wanted to learn her name. "You can talk all you want. Seriously this place is not safe. It really isn't." Zack then said, "I'm sure it's just another imagination you don't need to worry about." "Zack, but I'm really serious right now. I'm not imagining anything; I swear on my life something's going to and will happen!" No one listened to me. I sat in fear, waiting for the bad thing. An hour passed and people were still drinking and drunk out of their minds. "Vanessa, look around you nothing is wrong. Well, other than the drunkies drinking beer after beer." I was too frightened to answer. I had my knees together held by my arms.

Then, it happened.

"A fire!" One of the guys screamed from the kitchen. He ran out without his sneakers and part of his pants were burnt. I made my attention to Destiny for only a second. "I told you." I looked at the fire and back at her. "Let's get out of here." Destiny followed every order I said. "What do we do now?" "Go get Zack and bring him with us." Destiny saw that he was still with his girlfriend. "What about Courtney?" I huffed. "Do whatever you please. I just don't feel like being cooked tonight." People were screaming, some were even getting burned. Somehow the cops were called and they all got in trouble for the beer; except for Destiny, Zack, Courtney, and I. We were on our way to the roof. "Ok, we're going to jump." "What?" They all said. I tried to make them feel better about it. "It could be fun, feeling the breeze through your body, and the feeling like being on a rollercoaster. The only thing you have to worry about is crushing a few bones that's all. Who's ready?" They stared at me and just stared and stared with nothing to say.

"No one's going anywhere." We all swirled around to find a guy wearing a black mask and he was kind of tubby. "Who_" Destiny began to say but he interrupted. "Shut up! I didn't ask for you to speak." He rushed over and grabbed Zack. "Give him back!" I screamed. He jerked up to me. He got out a gun and put it to Zack's head. "You're lucky it's not your night to die yet. Now, one more word from you and I swear I will shoot this boy right here and now!" I zipped my mouth shut. A helicopter came over the roof. I couldn't tell who was driving it. I know for sure that it wasn't a cop. He then hopped onto the helicopter with Zack and they were gone into the slim darkness.

The Newspaper

I checked the mailbox when I got home to see if we had gotten anything and there was a newspaper inside. I went into the house and plopped on the chair in the kitchen to read it over. I saw an article on the front page; it was about my teacher that was missing today. The title read, "Death of Local High School Teacher, Mrs. Barley." It was last night when she died. Last night? Could you believe it? Who would just take away someone's sweet life just like that? That really isn't acceptable. She was at her boss' house discussing Social Studies, when she went into the bathroom and never came out. Her boss had quoted, "I heard a noise coming from the bathroom. It sounded like someone was getting murdered, so I went to find out what was going on." He knocked on the door maybe six times and no one answered. "Hello? Mrs. Barley, are you okay in there?" He still didn't get an answer. "Mrs. Barley, this is no time for games! If you're okay, tell me now." He realized the door was unlocked and gradually he opened the door slowly as he walked in. There was water all over the floor and blood coming out of the faucet.

He went over to the tub to see what was inside it. It was also filled with blood, but no sign of Mrs. Barley. "I didn't know where she was. I thought she disappeared but, boy, was I wrong." He told the police. The door was closing and that's when he got a surprise. Something hard hit him on the shoulder. It was like climbing a humongous mountain all the way to the very top in the middle of a snowstorm. He spun around to find her corpse lying in his hands. There was blood all over her and she looked different, scary looking. "I thought I was going to pass out." The article ended with the question, "What is going on?"

I then remembered the man at school who subbed for Mrs. Barley. I thought that maybe he had something to do with her death. I also wondered why he had been staring at Zack, Destiny, and I.

That night I had a nightmare. I dreamt that I was home alone and that was when I got a phone call. I answered and the voice on the other side was a whisper. The person said, "You will die soon." "Who is this?" I asked. There was no answer and the phone went dead. A guy walked in the room, he was even scarier than the sub at school and I could barely see his face. He said, "I told you I would get my revenge and kill you." I tried to run but he had a knife and he was right behind me. He grabbed my shoulder, I tried pulling my arm away but I couldn't, he was too strong for me. I saw that he had a switchblade in his pocket so I reached for it. At the same time, he stabbed my left arm, it was bleeding heavily. You could see blood dripping on the floor. I ran faster, out of breath. He tried to cut my neck open, but I took his switchblade and stabbed his leg. I stopped because out of nowhere came Zack. The man grabbed him, pulled him into the closet, and killed him.

I woke up barely breathing. There was bleeding coming out of my mouth and I looked to find scratches all over my left arm. I got up and saw a piece of paper on the floor, another note. I picked it up and read: "It's me again. How do you like the pain? Are you missing your friend Zack?" I told you the next step was just around the corner. I'm getting closer." That's when I knew I had to do something.

The Search

Saturday was the day I began thinking of a plan. First of all, I don't know if this person knows me or not. I also need to find out what happened to Zack and if he's really okay this time. I needed Destiny's help with this. She had the right amount of spy stuff at her house because her dad used to be a cop fighting crime; until that night he died in a shooting. I called Destiny up instantly. "Hello?" "Hi. What are you doing?" I asked. "Not much." She replied. "I need to talk to you about stuff." "What stuff?" I explained to her that I had gotten another note and needed to find out who it was from. "So can I use the spy equipment you have?" I asked, hopeful. Destiny replied, "Okay, you can come over now and we'll look together."

When I got to Destiny's house it was 1:00 pm. We went right upstairs to her bedroom where the computer was. She was typing in all these different buttons and then told me to try putting in the code and see what comes up. After I typed it in, a lot of results came up.

There was a big list of people. The first one I saw was Marakey, Brian. I clicked his name and there was a list of things about him. I clicked on "Brian Gets Jumped." And this is what it said: Brian lives in Brooklyn. He always got beaten up. One day he was walking alone and noticed a car was following him. He ran to hide behind a dumpster. The car stopped and a group of guys got out. They were part of a gang. They came up behind Brian and slammed him against a building. One of the boys, whose name was Mike, took Brian and stabbed him with a pocket knife. Another boy kicked him in the stomach and then they all walked away in a horizontal line, leaving him curled up in a ball on the ground. Someone came up to him, it was his sister, Maria. She had a perfect life. No one ever hurt her and she was very pretty. That was why something had to be done with her.

I scrolled down and I clicked on more notes. It said: Maria Marakey is now dead and next is . . . It didn't finish. We heard a voice coming from the computer. Destiny raised the volume so we could hear it. The voice said, "Destiny, I know you're with Vanessa. Are you guys scared? I bet you guys are wondering what happened to Zack. Well, you'll find out on your own." It got quiet for a minute, then we heard a laugh and it said, "Tonight." And then it was gone.

"I wonder what he meant by tonight." "I don't know but we'll probably find out tonight." We both sat there and just talked and then we realized it was 7:50 pm. I got thirsty therefore I went downstairs to get a drink. The kitchen was small, but cute. There were two sinks and a red floor. I went to the refrigerator, which was big. I believe it was the biggest thing in there. I got my drink and went towards the stairs. Halfway up, the doorbell rang so I went and opened it. No one was there, hence I shut the door and turned around. As soon as I proceeded to do that, the doorbell rang once again. I went and answered for a second time, no one was there, but there was a package left on the ground. So what do I do? Do I pick it up? Should I leave it? I'm curious to know what's in that package. Finally, I decided I would bring it upstairs and show it to Destiny. It was black, red, and blue with a bow on top. We were too scared to open it at first because it didn't say who it was from, but eventually we got courageous and opened it.

Inside the package was an unusual box. Destiny opened it and found pictures of Zack, her, and I. there was a note, too. I could only read a couple of words, but I read, "I miss you guys . . . Zack . . . Gone . . . Watch out for . . . Bye." I put the note down. "This means he's safe, Destiny!" I told her. That's what I thought, but I was unfortunately wrong.

Closer to the Truth

I wanted to find out what the rest of the note said. "We need someone else to help us." Destiny announced. "Like who?" I asked her. "Doesn't your cousin know how to read stuff that no one else can?" "Yeah, I think." I responded. So, we called my cousin on her house phone, but we got no answer. We tried calling her cell phone and a scared voice answered the phone, "Hello?" "Hi Leslie, It's Vanessa." "I know." "Is everything okay? You sound scared." I said. "Everything's good, so what'd you call for?" Leslie asked. "You remember my friend, Zack, right? Well he's missing and I got a package tonight. There's a note I need you to help me with." "Uhm, well I don't think I can help you." She replied. I heard someone whisper to her. I asked her, "Who's there with you?" "No one." She answered quickly. "I actually talked to Zack five minutes ago, he's really bruised up. I told him to go to your house so he can tell you anything you want to know." "Okay, thanks. Bye." I said and hung up. Destiny and I were both shaky when we got off the phone.

Destiny came to sleep over my house. We waited an hour for Zack and then the phone rang, it was him. "Hi Zack! When are you coming?" . . . "What do you mean you're not coming?" I exclaimed. In a very scared voice, he said, "I don't even know where I am. There's very little space here. I think I'm in a closet in someone else's house." "What!" I shouted. There was a deep voice in the background, "Alright, your time is up!" "No wait!" Zack's voice speeded up by like a mile. "Vanessa, I have something I need to say, I only went out with Courtney to make you jealous I didn't think you'd like me back. Just know I always cared about you." I answered in a scratchy voice finishing his sentence. "Love you." We heard a piece of metal hit something six times and then the sound of Zack screaming. A voice came on, "I know where you are, Vanessa. Too bad yours and Destiny's friend is now dead."

We cried for hours. I had a feeling someone was out to get me, but who could it be?

My Big Bro's visit

We had fallen asleep in the chair from last night. Today was weird because nothing out of the ordinary happened. There was no news about someone else being murdered. Two weeks passed and, still, nothing happened. Destiny and I decided to lay off for a bit.

"What are we going to do today?" Destiny asked me. "We could go to the mall." I suggested, "Sure." We took Destiny's car to the mall. It was pretty crowded today. When we went into 2CUTE, there was a stuffed animal that looked familiar. I walked over to it to examine it more closely. "Yo, Destiny. I remember before Melissa died, she had a stuffed animal exactly like this. It was a stuffed Chihuahua with light brown hair, big black eyes, and it smelled like cotton candy.

We felt someone behind us. The person grabbed our shoulders and we whipped around so fast, we almost fell over. This was a big surprise, it was my big brother. "Oh my gosh! What are you doing here?" I asked him in shock. "I thought that since I'm off from college for two weeks, I could come surprise you and visit." "Wow, Andrew, you couldn't just call me?" "Nope. So whatcha got there?" "It's a stuffed animal. It looks a lot like the one Melissa had before she died." "What's it doing here?" Andrew asked, curiously. My voice was trembling as I said, "I don't know."

The lights went out. It was pitch black and you couldn't see a thing, but you could hear voices. Those voices didn't belong to either of the three of us, I knew that. Or, so, I thought.

There was laughing, an evil laugh, too. The lights were still out and I was scared. Someone pinched me and then the lights went back on. By the time I turned around, the stuffed animal was gone. Someone else was missing too, but whom? I turned to see if Destiny was still next to me, and she was. She had a look on her face as if nothing happened.

"Wasn't that scary?" I asked. "No, not really. I'm perfectly fine." She assured me. "The stuffed animal is missing . . . Wait, something isn't right here. Where's my brother?" "I'm not sure where Andrew is, but is that blood on the floor?" Destiny asked me. "Do you think he's dead?" Now I was even more scared First Melissa, then Zack, and now Andrew. The best part is, is Destiny seemed like she didn't even care.

Destiny started to giggle. "Why are you giggling?" I demanded an answer. "This isn't funny!" "No reason, I just think it's pretty funny that there's blood on the floor, yet his body is nowhere to be found." "That's not funny!" I yelled.

Then I saw a note. Oh how wonderful. Here I am thinking the notes are over with. The note was on the counter next to Destiny. She had on a straight face now. I took the note from the counter and started to unfold it. I saw in big, bold letters: "TURN AROUND." I nervously turned around and saw Andrew's body on the floor with blood all over him. "No!" I screamed. "He really is dead!" I moved closer to him and whispered in his ear, "Please, please be alive." Then I heard a giggle. "Andrew?" There was no answer. I turned to look at Destiny, she still had on a straight face. I started to say something to her, but I felt something poke me. I swirled back to Andrew and he had changed the position he was in. His eyes were now wide open and he was staring at me. I screamed and fell backwards. Destiny and Andrew were laughing their butts off; meanwhile I was angry and silent.

"Haha, we got you!" They both exclaimed. "I can't believe you fell for it!" Destiny said. "Well, it looked realistic with the lights going out, the note and the blood!" I screamed at them. They only started laughing again. "Dude, that wasn't blood all over me, it was ketchup!" Andrew proudly announced. "Wow, you guys scared me half to death!" "Yeah, sorry about that. We just thought it would be funny." They both said. "Yeah, yeah. Let's just go back to my house." I was cranky.

It took us an hour to get back because of traffic. We finally got back to my house and Andrew went upstairs to take a shower. He had to get that ketchup off him. Destiny and I went into the kitchen. "This is really weird." I said to her. There were five newspapers on the table. "What?" Destiny asked, confused. "I don't recall having all these newspapers on my table. In fact, I didn't even check the mail." Destiny picked one up and read it. "Uh, you're not gonna like this one." "What does it say?" She didn't answer me. "Destiny, c'mon, what does it say?" I pleaded.

My cell phone rang; I answered it. "Hello?" "Yeah, hi Vanessa, it's Leslie." "Oh, hi." I tried my best to sound annoyed. Here's the catch, it was actually working. "Uhm, is everything okay?" "Well, no actually I'm not. Let's see, why am I not okay? Oh yeah, that's right I know why. I had called Zack up to find out where he is, only to find out that Zack didn't know where he even was, and that he thought he was in someone else's closet. The next thing you know is, is that some guy kills him with some sort of metal!" "Oh, uh, I'm sorry about that. He must've gone to a different place on an accident or something. I didn't know . . ." I began to interrupt her, but she cut me off with her voice, low and scared. "It's back." She whispered. "What? I didn't quite comprehend what you said" "It's back." She repeated, again in a whisper. "What's back?" I asked, very confused. What is her game here? She was silent now. The sound of her heavy breathing made me sense a bad vibe. I had a strange feeling someone was threatening her, but I didn't ask her if she was or anything. Destiny held up the newspaper to show me what Leslie was blabbering about. The title read, "The Killer's Back and Ready to Kill." I stood there, with arms crossed, not saying one word.

The Incident in the Bathroom

There was screaming coming from the upstairs bathroom where Andrew was. He came running down the stairs out of breath. "What's wrong?" Destiny and I asked. "I saw something in the bathroom." I could see that there was blood dripping down his back. "This isn't another prank from you guys, is it?" "No I'm serious." Andrew said, "Follow me."

We went upstairs and stopped at the door, he opened it slowly as he told us what happened and warned us of the blood on the floor. Wow, it looks like World War two in here. If there's that much blood how is he possibly living? "I was in the shower washing my hair. While I was doing that I remembered that I forgot the body soap on the sink. As I was about to open the shower curtain something stopped me. It was a sound. Without moving a muscle, I listened with my ear closely only to hear the sound of the body soap falling onto the floor. I hesitated for a moment not knowing what I should do. After a few minutes I got the courage and took a peak out from my shower curtain and there was nothing there. All I saw was the body soap on the floor *in a changed position. I decided to* continue finishing my shower. Once I was done I got out. In matters of moments, I put on my boxers and took a look into the mirror; that's when I saw someone behind me." The tone of his voice changed and he began speaking faster. "It all happened so fast, I couldn't even see his face. I could only see the mask he wore, and the knife he had in his hand. The knife stood out more than his whole tubby body. He stabbed me in the back leaving me to suffer through blood flowing down my back. It stung really badly. I grabbed the soap and put it on top of the sink. Of course that's when I started screaming. He vanished out of nowhere and so then I ran down to you two."

"Wow. Things just keep getting weirder and weirder. Don't they? I can't even explain it." I said. "You wanna know what the strangest part is?" Destiny asked In wonder. "What?" Andrew and I both inquired. "Look inside the shower, do you guys notice the jacket over there? It has a number on it. Oh, and take a quick moment to view the crack in the window as well." "Hand over the jacket. I want to check it out." We brought the jacket downstairs to the living room. My eyes grew wide as I said, "It looks familiar." Unfortunately, Andrew and Destiny were acting like a pair of missing goggles. This meant I would have to explain it to them. "How is it possibly recognizable?" Andrew asked me. "Remember our cousin, Leslie?" "Yeah. How's she been anyway? I haven't heard from her in a long time." "Who cares about right now? Now, do you remember when we went to her house that one time when I was nine, you were twelve, and she was eight? Do you also remember her mom giving her a big black jacket?" He stared in confusion. "I can't say I do remember; it happened like seven or eight years ago. The only thing I remember is her crying to her mommy because some guy stole her ice cream cone."

"That's it? Out of everything that's the only thing you can dwell upon? Well, I guess that's fine I'll explain it you then. So, this is what happened. We were outside and it was cold out. I had on a sweatshirt, but she didn't she only had on a T-shirt. In such matter, her mom gave her a big black jacket. She said that she could keep it just in case she ever was cold again. The only difference between the two jackets is that the one Leslie had, has purple stains on the inside from grape juice." "Hmm, but there aren't any stains in this jacket." Destiny stated to us. "Or maybe there is . . ." I trailed off. I took it from Andrew and looked it over even more carefully. After consideration, I at last saw it. The small stain was hiding inside the jacket near a pocket. "There it is! I think we should give Leslie a call and invite her over." I shouted as I walked over to the kitchen. I was definitely the complete opposite from happy, rather frantic. After I got off the phone with Leslie, I came back to Andrew and Destiny. "Okay, she's coming now. Put the jacket on the floor next to you, Destiny." I ordered.

We sat on the couch and watched TV for a while until the doorbell rang. "I'll get it." Andrew told us. They both walked back to the living room. "Hi." Destiny and I said. I went and turned off the TV. "You can sit down." I told her with attitude. "Okay." Her voice was shaky as she sat across from us. "I have a question for you." I said. "What?" "Would you like to explain this?" Destiny handed me the jacket from the floor. "I don't know what you're talking about." She told us. "Yes, you do. This jacket is yours. It even has the purple stain in it." I showed her the spot on the inside. "I remember the jacket; I just don't know what you're talking about." Destiny obviously wanted to say something, so I let her. "It was left upstairs in the shower." We all stared at Leslie in silence. She looked serious, her face wasn't even red. "You really don't know how it got here?" Leslie didn't say anything.

"Did you know that Andrew got stabbed in the back?" "No!" Leslie was getting mad. "I don't know anything about this!" She yelled. There was complete silence again. Out of nowhere, a door slammed shut upstairs. The lights dimmed and you could only see a little. "What's going on?" I demanded an answer. "I don't know." Leslie simply replied back. "I'll go see what's up there." Andrew suggested. "Be careful, you're already hurt enough." I reminded him. "I will."

"I'm confused." Destiny was talking to Leslie. "I mean, how did your jacket even get here? And without you even knowing about it, either?" I was studying Leslie's face and she looked like she was getting nervous. Then, we heard something get knocked against something else.

Carved

"Maybe I should leave now." Leslie suggested. I pointed my finger at her. "No. You stay right there." Destiny and I started going up the stairs. It was really dark, the lights upstairs weren't working. We went through the hall slowly and heard someone whispering to us. It was a girl's voice. "You will pay and your brother will be dead." "What was that?" Destiny asked, just as afraid as I was. I didn't show it that much, it was all on the inside. "Help me!" We heard Andrew's weak voice. "Where are you?" I called out to him. "I'm in your room." I walked over to my room to find that my door was locked. We heard a person slam him up against the door and tell him to shut up. "What is going on?" "I don't know." I was wondering the same thing. We were quiet so we could hear what was going on. I was beyond scared now because Andrew was the only person that understood and cared for me. My parents were barely ever home and I didn't get presents for my birthday or Christmas. But I was okay with it, except, now, I wasn't too sure about it.

We heard the wind blow fiercely and now it was raining pretty badly out. Five minutes passed and everything was quiet. I tried opening the door again, it was unlocked. I slowly opened and all you could hear was the sound of it creaking, until it got stuck. We both pushed it, it wouldn't budge. Destiny tried again by herself. She went back and ran into it. It busted open and she went flying and landed on her butt. The only light was from the moon coming in through the window. No one was there. "Do you see Andrew?" I asked. "No, but I'm really scared." Someone was coming; I could hear the creaking of the steps. All of a sudden the door slammed shut and there was a person behind us, staring. We were glancing at the corner of our eyes. She was a girl with dark black hair and some white in it. She looked like she could be sixteen or seventeen. Her face was pale white and she had a cut on her face. She was wearing all grey and had on white shoes.

Destiny and I stood there as motionless as two statues. The girl came closer to us with a big, sharp knife pointing downward in her hand. Destiny started to move up and then stopped. All you heard now was the girl's heavy breathing. She moved behind Destiny, grabbed her arm, and held the knife to her. Destiny went down to the floor in pain, but she wasn't bleeding. She only had a cut. The girl pushed us out of the way and went into the closet.

In a cold and scared voice, Destiny whispered to me, "Who was that?" As she got up. Yes, because I know every scary pale girl on this planet. "How should I know? But let's find out." We opened the closet door and the girl wasn't there, but Andrew was. He was lying against the wall with his head down. Blood was dripping down his arms to the floor. I went and lifted his head. "Aye, look at this. Dude, this is messed up." I pointed to what I was talking about. "It is." There was writing on his forehead in marker with the words, "revenge 666."

Andrew was dead now, but who killed him? I thought I would never find out, but I did.

Alone

We heard a voice say something to us. We turned around and it was Leslie. "You were supposed to be waiting downstairs on the couch." "I heard a noise so I came up here," Leslie said. I showed Leslie what happened to Andrew. It looked like we were all about to cry. I started to and then Destiny did. Leslie was just staring at us. Now it was four in the morning, the sky was cloudy and it was still raining. We went downstairs for a bit and talked and for a little while, nothing bad happened.

The phone rang and Destiny answered, she got no response. "Hey guys, I'm going to put the phone on speaker so we can all hear." We all looked down at the phone. We knew someone was on the other line because it showed up on the caller ID. "Look, we know someone's there, okay?" There was still no answer. "Okay, who is this and why aren't you answering us?" Three minutes later, someone finally answered. The voice wasn't soft at all, it was rough and scary. "I want what's mine."

He demanded. "What the heck are you talking about?" "Oh, you know what I'm talking about Vanessa." I stared at Leslie and Destiny and they returned the stare. I replied, "What do you mean by that?" Once again, no response and the phone went dead.

It was beginning to thunder and lightning out now and Leslie and Destiny were right behind me. I stood there staring at the phone. "You guys heard what he said?" "Yeah." Without looking behind me to see their faces, I asked them, "Do you two think something bad is going to happen to you both?" I got no answer. "Destiny? Leslie?" Still, I got no answer. I put the phone on its hook and heard noises. It sounded like someone was trying to get my attention but they couldn't because their mouth was covered with something. Then the noise stopped. I slowly turned and began screaming. The girl from upstairs was sitting on the couch right in front of me. Still screaming, a flash of lightening occurred and she was gone. Leslie and Destiny were gone too. Now I was alone. Isn't that just great?

Hunting

There was a crack in the two windows. The one on the right had a post-it note with writing on it. I took it under the lamp and read it. "I've talked to Destiny and Leslie. Were at The Haunts Mansion and I'm not alone, someone else is helping me out. I'm getting my revenge and you have five days, or else . . ."

Who could that be? I have to find them. I only get five days, or else. What will the person do if I don't make it on time? Tomorrow will be day one.

Today was Tuesday and there was school, but I decided to skip this week. I kept looking back at the note. I remembered back on the code that Mr. Spike was discussing with the man. Since the code only worked on Destiny's computer, I went to her house. It was actually sunny out. That's something different. The last few days were cloudy.

The only thing that didn't change was the wind. It was still blowing in my face as usual.

I reached her house after walking there. There was a car in the driveway. I went through the back. There was a glass door to get in. It was locked so I had to knock a few times. Destiny's sister came to the door to open it. "Hi Vanessa." Her voice was kind of high pitched and sweet. "Hey," I said quickly as I walked right by her. "Where's Destiny?" "Uhm . . ." There was a long pause. "She got kidnapped . . ." "What! Oh my, we have to call the police!" I told her no but she went to the phone anyway. It rang as soon as she put her hand on it. She had a scared look on her face so I told her to put it on speaker. The voice was a sweet, girl's voice, but scary at the same time. She said, "I know who you guys are." We listened to what the girl was saying, then the voice turned into a deep manly one. "If you guys call the police, you're going to wish you never did. Remember, Vanessa, I have Leslie and your little friend." The voice went back to the girl's voice. "Okay, now be careful girls," she laughed and hung up.

We were both shaking. "Kelsey, can I use the computer?" "Why?" "I know a way to get Destiny back, and Leslie, too." "Fine. As long as I get to go up there, too." "Okay. You can, but can you get me a drink first?" "Sure. I'm kind of thirsty myself. I'll be up in five minutes." "Alright," I called as I went upstairs to Destiny's room. It was really messy. I pushed some clothes off the chair and sat down. I put everything in that Destiny and I had done last time. A whole bunch of numbers camp up. It went by so fast, then it stopped at the end of the page. I typed in the code and got onto the page I had seen. I looked at all the results, found the right one and clicked on it.

Kelsey came in with the drinks. "So, did you find anything yet?" Kelsey was pretty. She had brown hair with red highlights. Her eyes were bulish green and her clothes were pretty, too. "Not yet. I'm typing it in now." I took a sip of my drink and it was good. It was fruit punch, I love fruit punch.

I tried typing in The Haunts Mansion. I got a lot of information on it. "Yes! There's the address! Kelsey, get me a piece of paper and a pen!" "Okay." She went in the other room to find a pen and then came back and bent over to the bottom drawer to get paper. She had on a half shirt, and I saw something on her lower back. I took a closer look at it. It was a big, red scar that looked like someone's nails dug into her skin. She got up quickly, so I looked away as fast as I could. She handed me the paper and I wrote down the address.

On my Own

I had only four days left. I had fallen asleep on the chair and decided to look up the thing Kelsey had on her lower back. Frist, I went to go see where she was. She was sleeping on the couch downstairs and was snoring very loud. I went back to the room and looked it up. "Oh my god . . ." I whispered to myself. It meant that Kelsey had a nightmare that seemed real where two people hurt her.

I heard footsteps coming, it was Kelsey. She didn't look too good. She had a glass cup in her hand, it was empty, too, which was weird. Her eyes looked evil and she was breathing heavy. She took a step closer to me without saying a word. She held up the glass cup and was now hovering over me. Then she dropped the glass and backed away. Some of the glass shattered and cut my arm. I went to the bathroom to get a towel to put around it and then went back to find Kelsey. Her face turned a nice, cream brown to pale white and her body was shaking. She dropped to the floor and started choking. I went to help her but she dug her nails into my neck. I pushed her arm away and backed off. She was coughing really hard. She put both of her hands on her neck and pushed up. Then her eyes turned inwards and she was bleeding from her nose.

Out of nowhere, the door slammed shut. I turned around, but no one was there. I moved my head downwards and there it was at my feet coming from Kelsey, and it was heading towards the door. I tried opening it but it was locked from the outside. I banged on the door. "Who's out there? Open this door right now!" I was screaming. I stopped to see if anyone would respond. Right then and there was the laughter of the girl that was on the phone. I banged on the door again. "Why are you doing this?" I was still screaming. She answered, "I warned you about trying to get in contact with the police." Before she could go on, I interrupted her. "We never even tried to call the police!" There was laughter. "Maybe you didn't, but she did. And for that, it's just a matter of time before she dies." Then the girl's voice stopped. "Wait! What do you mean?" Silence. "Hello? Are you still there? Answer me if you are!" Still, silence. I turned back to Kelsey, she was still alive and whispering something to me. "What?" "Be careful at The Haunts Mansion." Those were Her last words before she died, and now I was on my own. Oh Great, just great.

Journey to the Haunts Mansion

Today I started walking to The Haunts Mansion. I got out of Destiny's house as quick as I could. I never really liked it because it always looked scary there. Day three went by fast. It was already midnight so I stopped walking because I was exhausted. There was music playing in the morning, that's what woke me up. I was hungry so I stopped at the deli to get some food. There were a lot of blacks and Latinos. I know I have some Latina in me, but not a lot. I have more French in me. I had to wait fifteen minutes after I ordered. I sat down and looked around. Everyone was staring at me, so I stared at the wall. "Hey you," a voice said. I turned around. Fifteen minutes were up. "Get your lazy butt over here." The guy had a nasty attitude. "You don't have to get all nasty with me." Some people started getting up and coming towards me. The guy put his hands into a fist. "Whatcha say kid?" "Nothing. I didn't mean anything, you're a very nice person." I struggled on the 'nice' part. He handed me the food and gave me back my change. "Now, where ya headin' kid?" "Uhm, The Haunts Mansion." There were gasps

all over the room. "You betta watch ya self, kid. It's dangerous dere."
"My friends got taken there." More gasps. "The killer took 'em, huh?
I'm warning you, be careful dere, ya hear?" I didn't answer him. Some
kid behind me said, "He asked you something. You answer whenever
someone asks you something. Now, answer him!" I forced myself to say,
"Uh, yeah. I hear." I ran out of there. I started eating while I walked
away. People on the streets were giving me mean looks as I walked by. I
kept on seeing the girl, but when I blinked she wasn't there.

It was eight o'clock at night now. I looked up and saw the sign that
read The Haunts Mansion, seven hours. I was getting cold and I was
shivering. I remembered the chilling laughter of the girl. It sounded
familiar, like I knew the person from somewhere. I figured it couldn't
be, a lot of people love me. But, dude. I was so wrong.

Arrived

On Friday I finally arrived. The mansion had big gates. It was storming out; thunder and lightening. I stepped towards the gate and it opened. There were tree branches all over the ground and I kept stepping on them. It was scary because the whole time I felt like someone was following me. The steps were hard to get up. There were maybe ten steps to go and my legs were killing me.

I was about to knock on the door, when it swung open on its own. I guess they knew I was here. The floors creaked as I walked. It looked old and scary. There was blood on every wall. I went looking for Destiny and Leslie on the main floor. I didn't find them in the living room, so I checked the kitchen. I walked slowly, then stopped. I saw the refrigerator door was open and somebody's legs were showing. I moved slowly to the kitchen. I hid next to the stove and squatted down. The refrigerator door slammed shut and a big, scary guy stood there. "Who's in here?" He shouted. I didn't answer him. His voice sounded familiar though. I swore it was like I knew him from somewhere. I couldn't see his face though.

He walked away with a sand-which in one hand and a pointy object in the other. I followed him to the basement. I hid behind a big, wide, brown box. It was so dark until he put on a dim light. Then I saw his face. Why does he look so familiar? I think I know him but I'm not sure. Someone grabbed my foot and pulled me closer to them. "What's going on?" I murmured. I sat up and out of the corner of my eye, I saw somebody was sitting next to me, laughing. I looked closer. "Ahhh!" I screamed. It was the girl. I tried getting up but she wouldn't let me. My arm was stinging like crazy and I realized I was bleeding again. "Where are my friend and cousin?" I shouted. "Shut up!" The guy yelled back in the darkness. He put on a brighter light and I saw Destiny and Leslie. "Help!" They pleaded. "Let us go!" Leslie looked scared to death. Destiny had blood gushing out of her mouth. They were behind bars like they were in jail, but they really weren't.

The girl started talking. "Ha. I know you don't like this . . ." My heart was pounding and I jumped when she whispered in my ear. "But I had to get my revenge." "What are you talking about?" I asked. She was quiet. She got up to turn all the lights on. She shook her head, pulled all her hair in front of her face, and then flipped it back. "Chenelle?" "Shut up! I don't need to hear your mouth." Chenelle was my sister, but Andrew and I never really talked to her much. One day, she was just gone and we didn't notice until now. But I never thought she would hate us like this. "Why are you . . . ?" I stopped because she had something behind her back. "What do you have behind your back?" I asked. Then she pulled out a gun and pointed it at me. Destiny and Leslie were horrified.

Leslie was on the floor hysterically crying, "I'm so sorry, Vanessa! I didn't know all of this was going to happen!" "Wuh?" I was puzzled. "I thought you said you didn't have anything to do with his? That you didn't do anything wrong?" Chenelle joined our conversation. "Oh, but she did have something to do with this. She's been helping me out this whole time on where you were and what you guys were doing." Then Leslie said, "Yeah. So what? I did, but then I had nothing to do with it when you said you were going to kill Andrew!" Leslie was angry behind her tears. "Shut up!" Chenelle screamed and pointed the gun at Leslie. She shot her in the leg and now she was bleeding. "Aye, you don't have to get so mad and get all mean like that," Destiny said. Chenelle saw Destiny still had blood gushing from her mouth when she talked. All she did was threaten her with the gun, she didn't shoot. Destiny went quiet. Chenelle pointed the gun back at me. I tried getting away but the big guy came up behind me and held me tight so I couldn't get away. "Who are you?" I asked him. "He's your uncle. Ya know, the one who was in jail," Chenelle explained to me with a smirk on her face. I replied, "Uncle Bob?" "Yeah, child?" "How did you get out?" I questioned with a little anger in my voice.

Chenelle started laughing. She dimmed the lights and continued talking. "You see, let me tell ya a little story. I would always be with you guys for every frickin' thing. Like church, I was there. Easter, I was there. At last, I got tired of it. I went to clean my room and I remembered you would order me to clean yours. You threatened me that if I didn't, you would tell everyone about the whole teacher incident. So, I did whatever you wanted. Until one day, I ran away thinking you guys would come after me. But, you didn't." Chenelle was furious. "I'm sorry," I told her. "I'm not finished yet." I said no more and let her proceed. "I was walking the streets by myself when someone grabbed me and scratched my forehead. That's why I have this scar." She showed me. "It was Uncle Bob. He told me he broke out of jail and he hated our family, especially you. He explained to me how he wanted his revenge, so we went up to our parents' business meeting and killed them in their hotel room." I was getting upset and angry that he had killed my parents, when Chenelle pointed the gun to my head.

Home at Last

At that moment, I did a flip backwards, knocking the gun out of her hand and letting me loose of Uncle Bob's grip. The gun went flying across the room. Destiny heard and saw everything that was going on. Leslie was passed out by now. I went for the gun and so did Uncle Bob. Chenelle was on the floor because I had kicked her halfway across the room. She tried to get up. I got the gun before my uncle, and he backed off when he saw me point it at him. I knew I had scared him, so I turned towards Chenelle.

I heard heavy footsteps come up behind me. I spun around and it was him coming at me with a knife. I was panicking. I didn't know what to do, so I shot him. I knew it wasn't right, and I felt bad, but I had no choice. I couldn't get away. He was dead and there was a lot of blood where I shot him. I didn't cry. I looked back to where Chenelle was, but she wasn't there. I couldn't find her, but it didn't matter to me because I had to get Leslie and Destiny to the hospital. I went over to the bars to let them out. They were in really bad shape. I found the button to open it and pushed it.

We were at the hospital. I was talking to the doctor while they were in the emergency room. The doctor assured me they would be out in anywhere from four to seven weeks. I said okay, thanked him, and left for home. It took me an hour to walk back. Everything was good. Or, so, I thought.

Uncle Bob was dead, Chenelle was nowhere to be found, and Destiny and Leslie were going to be just fine. Then I got a phone call. "Hello?" There was only breathing. "Hello, is anyone there?" Then there was a slight laughter, and the phone went dead. I wasn't that worried about the call; probably just somebody feeling the sudden urge to do a prank call. I went up to my room and sat down on my egg chair. I remembered the first night I got the note. It was cold and windy and I heard someone at my door. Well, I had the same feeling tonight. I didn't turn around. Then the door opened a little bit. My heart was racing. I turned around and opened the door. I looked out of it. No one was there. I went back to my chair and sat down again. I could feel someone was standing behind me. I went to turn around but their hand covered my mouth and the other one covered my eyes so I couldn't see. Their nails started to dig into my skin. I felt blood running down my cheek.

The Mirror

The next thing I knew was that I wasn't home. If I wasn't home, then where the heck am I? I had woken up to the sound of eccentric music and the slight sound of raindrops trickling down the window next to me. There was a mirror on the other side of the room, I decided I wanted to go up to it and see how bad my cheeks were scarred. It was a horrible idea going up to it. The mirror felt ice cold and sent a shiver up my spine. I stepped closer to it and stepped into a puddle of red, nauseating blood. Taking another look at the mirror, there was a tiny crack in it. I touched the crack of the mirror and examined it closely. The mirror started to open and rift. Wasn't that a pleasant surprise? I quickly proceeded to step away and the glass shattered all over the floor; bits and pieces scattered here and there. Luckily I didn't get scratched up again. I looked up at the mirror once again with a puzzled expression on my face. In it there was a dark hallway. What's this, a dark hallway? Should I step into it? Taking a deep breath, I walked in.

Every single step I took made a noticeable noise. Then that's when I heard little voices, I stopped instantly. Crap, What if these voices are out to get me? I'm not in the mood for anymore drama. But does that stop anyone? No, it does not. As my paranoia continued, the voices continued and I wanted to see where they were coming from. Were they conversing or bickering? If conversing, what were they possibly conversing about? I surely hope not about me. Like I pointed out before I dealt with enough drama. Anyways, I listened for the voices. It appeared to be that they were coming from a little room with the door shut and locked.

I looked around me and everything was obscure that i could barely see no figure out where I am. This certainly wasn't a fun adventure as like going to six flags or even the Maldives! Staring at the door, I put my ears up to it to listen to the voices. The voices were indeed conversing; "We're dead there's nothing we can do about it." "But Jason we need to help her! We have got to find a way!" "I know M . . ." The Jason kid didn't finish the name. "There's someone here I can smell it" Jason said harshly. As angry as he sounds I would assume he's crinkling his nose.

Quickly, I backed away from the door. I started running through puddles of water and the same exact nauseating blood. Jason still had his voice harsh. "Who is disturbing us? Get your butt over here! Jason was beyond angry that someone was disturbing them.

As I was running, I was thinking about the girl that was with Jason. Her voice sounded like she wasn't that old, perhaps somewhere around my age. Jason was still yelling and it sounded like he was right behind me. So, I looked behind me and all I see is a little white dot from a distance. That must be him. Eh, he's not that close as I thought he would be. Unfortunately when I turned back around I saw a train coming at me.

Imagination

Home? Since when did I get here? Wasn't I just in front of a train? I apparently was confuzzled(confused and puzzled). I didn't get why I was home when I was just in front of a train. Oh well. I'm probably hallucinating.

My intentions were to sit down and watch TV. Instead, I went to the kitchen to see if there was anything worth eating. I rummaged around to find fig newton bars, cheese nips, and sour cream and onion chips; nothing that pertained my interest. The usual wild cherry coke and extra buttery popcorn is the way to go. It was cold inside my house, especially in the kitchen for some odd reason. Upon opening the refrigerator door, I felt a shiver go down my back. I had gotten a little scared but didn't panic. Then that's where it all began, I heard screaming.

My heart started pounding fast and something grabbed my foot. I jumped and turned around with disbelief. When I turned around I saw a body, a dead body. I took a closer look and it was Zack. Now I was screaming too, along with the screaming that I heard. "Zack?" I asked. His hand grabbed my ankle tighter. "Ow Zack! Stop that!" I said a little loud and then I blinked a couple of times. Out of nowhere, Zack vanished and the lights popped and went out. Was I dreaming of this? Was Zack really there? Did someone put it there? Well, if that's the darn case, how on earth did they get in?

It was dark inside my house now. I tried finding my way to the living room couch; the floors kept creaking as I walked slowly, cautiously. Finally, I got to the couch and it felt weird. As I sat, still cautious, there was the breathing of someone else going into my ear. "What's going on?" I whispered to myself with a frightened tone.

The TV then turned on; I stared at it to see what would proceed to happen. There was still breathing going into my ear, then I heard a whisper. "What now?" I said in a low, demoralized voice. There was no answer, not even sight or sound of one. I looked to the right of me and found that my remote was there. So I picked up the remote, looking at the remote I felt someone grab my neck. What could possibly be happening to me now? Well, whoever it was started choking me; I found it very hard to breathe. Shaking, struggling to get up I couldn't.

A picture came onto the screen of the TV. It was a picture of two girls and a man with a knife, similar to a machete knife. The volume was on too, but the people weren't saying anything. They were just moving. I was still getting choked, and I saw the man with the knife go stab one of the girls. So I tried looking away, but I couldn't. The man stabbed the other girl and she was dead. Then he looked towards me and said, "It's your turn." "No!" I screamed. The knife came through the TV, pointing at me. Blood was dripping down from the knife on to the floor. It was making me sick at the sight. "Leave me alone!" I shouted. A smirk came upon the guy's face, no one was choking me anymore. I finally could breathe normally; I was still staring at the screen, the knife dropped and the screen went blank. The lights turned back on. I remained still just staring at the knife. Finally, I got up and went over to the knife. I just left it there, not knowing and definitely not wishing to know what would happen if I touched it. What if I was hallucinating again? Has my paranoia really gotten the best of me?

It's morning now and I thought I was dreaming everything that happened yesterday night. I felt lazy, so I twisted and turned for fifteen minutes in my bed; until the sun really decided to shine through my window. As I got up, I ran my fingers through my hair and looked outside at the remaining puddles of last night's rain. I went to the bathroom to freshen up. While I was getting ready for the day, I was singing TIK TOK it's pretty catchy. I started washing my face and then looked up into the mirror. There was a face staring at me. So I blinked a few times and then it was gone.

After I finished getting ready I went to my room. I tried to recall the face I saw in the mirror. I needed a clip that matched my outfit and began looking through my drawers for one. As I was looking I noticed that I had the bloody knife on top of my dresser. Where did this come from? Didn't I leave this downstairs? I looked around my room to see any other disturbing things. Luckily, nothing crossed me yet.

Secrets

Destiny and Leslie came over around 4 o'clock. "Hey guys!" I was excited to see them. "Yo!" they both said. "So you two are finally out of the hospital, huh!" "Yep. We're as good as can be." Leslie said. "Hmm" Destiny said sliding into the kitchen, "How are things going around here with you? Anything new perhaps?" I didn't say anything. In fact, I was speechless. What was there to say? Frankly, it was quite difficult to explain every detail to them. While I was deep in thought Destiny tried getting my attention by calling out my name. "Vanessa?" Destiny's lightly shaded brown eyebrows raised while her head titled a little over towards the left.

I left Destiny and Leslie hanging in the kitchen. Meanwhile I went upstairs to get the knife, without a word of reply. It was so cold in my room and not only because it was winter, but because of something peculiar. My room was a freezer. The chills ran down my back as I walked further into the room. The knife was just laying there with the dry blood on it. I wrinkled my nose at the sight of it. I walked up to the knife and there was a tiny note attached to it. "Have fun tonight . . ." What's this all about? And why does it appear to be a different color each time I get a note? This time the color is white crayon but on a black piece of paper. I surely do not like notes at all. They are nothing but issues to me.

I took the knife and note down the stairs with me. As I was walking down, I heard Leslie and Destiny talking in a low tone. Instantly I stopped walking to listen to their conversation. "No we can't tell her." "But why can we not? Vanessa is my best friend and your cousin? It just wouldn't be right." "It doesn't matter, do you know how much danger we will be in if we tell her!? We got to just keep our cool and look unsuspicious." Leslie sounded a little bit tense and not as much of the worried part. "Yeah, I know how much danger we'll be in, but c'mon Leslie I don't know how much longer I can keep this secret from Vanessa. I can try and not appear to look like I'm being devious but I just don't know if can pull that off." Destiny sounded like she wanted to burst out into tears. "Hah, what are you talking about we just saw Vanessa today? You can totally pull it off, but whatever you do, do not end up jumpy." "Eh, I'll try not to and yeah that's true. I did only see her today." Destiny and Leslie giggled a little bit and then stopped. "When she comes, follow my lead." Leslie directed to Destiny.

'Follow my lead?' What does she mean by this? "Hum." I said coming down the stairs to let them know I was soon to be entering the kitchen where they were. On my way down, I heard Leslie and Destiny shuffling themselves into chairs. When I entered the kitchen they were just staring at me like nothing happened between them. Both of them had fear in their eyes as I held the note and the bloody knife behind my back. "What's that behind you?" Leslie asked. The expressions on their faces were like they already knew what it was, but they were trying to pull it off as if they were unaware of the situation at hand. "Umm." I pulled out the knife and note from behind my back. "What's the note say?" I handed Destiny the note and her and Leslie both read it out loud. They both looked at each other with worry. "Weird ay?" I said wondering what they would say, implying it in a tone that I knew that they would know something I didn't. "Oh, yeah, it totally is." It seemed like they weren't so surprised at it as much as I was.

"So what do you think about the knife?" I questioned, suspiciously. Again they looked at each other with a secretive look and then back at me. Without saying a word I gave them a mistrustful look and set the knife down on the counter. Well, aren't they doing a great job keeping it cool? "Are you guys' fine? You seem a little . . . edgy." "Yes!" Leslie said a little too loudly realizing that I was on to them. "Maybe!" Destiny said also a little too deafeningly. "Ok chillax(chill and relax combined) I was just wondering. I'm allowed to have curiosity's you know." I was starting to get a little irritated at the two of them.

"Hey, what do you say we all go to the ice skating rink?" Leslie changed the subject in a flash. She leaned back and nudged Destiny in the rib. A sound of pain made its way through Destiny's mouth. Holding her right side with her hand, she hopped up to stand adjacent to Leslie and crosswise from me. "Yeah, Vanessa let's go!" I began poking the top of the knife with my pointer finger. For some reason the knife wasn't as sharp as I thought it would have been. While twirling the knife around and taking closer glimpses of it, the other two shifted back heading near the door. At the corner of my eye I spotted the faucet. Perfect. I hustled over to the faucet and ran the knife from end to end. Dumbfounded I pulled the knife from the water to find that the blood didn't come off. An Idea suddenly popped into my head. Quickly I opened up the widely lengthen cabinets underneath the faucet and searched for a wipe. Finally, I came across Lysol wipes and stretched for them. Good, three more left to use. Aggressively, I scrubbed the dry blood off; it fell into the garbage can in chunks. At a slow pace numbers came up from the shiny knife. One, three, two. Whatever did this mean? "Vanessa?" Once again my name was being called from Destiny, "Are you coming or not?" Throwing the knife in the sink I said, "Most certainly."

As we arrived with scarfs, baggy sweatpants, hats, and jackets . . . I couldn't help but think that it was the middle of winter and were entering an ice box. "Welcome to the ice skating rink I see there's three of you, your total is going to be thirty-five dollars and twenty-three cents." We all digged into our pockets taking out all the money we had on us. After we sorted the price in half, we headed over to the skates and put them on. My eyes were peeled onto Leslie and Destiny exchanging looks. I thought that was mine and Destiny's thing. Guess it wasn't anymore or maybe their merely keeping another secret from me. I seriously did not like what I was seeing. "Okay! Let's skate!" Destiny cheered as her and Leslie began skating away without me. "Yeah, guys, maybe your forgetting that I don't really know how to skate!" forget it. They can't hear me.

I twisted and turned leaning against the bars in the rink, grasping to keep grip of them as I took a wrong turn and fell flat on my butt. While striving to get back up, I felt my hands come across writing carved into the ice. I squinted my eyes to read it, and considering the fact of people skating it made it a tad harder to read. It give the impression that it was a sentence. It had read: Still hitting the ice I see? I thought you quit ice skating the first time when you ended up in the hospital? Guess not. Is it a bad thing that your tag is sticking out of your jacket? Oh, and another thing, why are Leslie and Destiny not with you? Did they finally realize what a selfish jerk you are? I mean look at them have a good time without you. They didn't even come over to see if your bleeding; although you're nowhere near bleeding . . . oh wait, is that a little blood I spot with my little eyes on your right hand?

I flew up as fast as possible. Everyone was laughing and having a blast but me. As usual I became worried and afraid. I sluggishly whirled around me to find a girl with black hair and bangs that covered one of her eyes. I believe she was an emo girl. Anyways, she glared at me with a plain face. Without thinking I marched up to her to find a white crayon in her hands. "Excuse-me but where'd you get that crayon?" I slightly curiously asked. The girl glanced at the crayon and then back at me. "I got it where any other girl like me would've gotten it from." "Like where?" "Well, don't you like asking questions. Maybe I should ask you a pile of questions." She stated, "But if you must know, I got it from my friend. I did have a red crayon, but it didn't seem to fit my style. That's why I had to get rid of it. You know, toss it out? It's like throwing a dead body into the dumpster to erase the evidence." She evilly smirked. I stared at her thinking of a question to ask. Hmm, well she was glaring at me; maybe I should ask her why she likes staring at people. "Well, hey, why were you glaring at me before?" The girl put her white crayon in her throw on bag. "I didn't know that staring at someone was a felony. I guess I broke the law over a million of times already." Her facial expression was so angry that I thought she was ready to shank me. "What is your name?" I asked ignoring her statement. "Dead meat." "What?" "Did I stutter? Or do you need to get your ears checked? Dead. Meat."

Leslie and Destiny rushed over to Vanessa. "Vanessa! Mr. Spike is here! The one that you heard give that man the code!" "Should I go say hi to him?" Leslie and Destiny became hushed. Leslie said, "Uh . . . well, if you want to you can . . . Vanessa, do you really think that's a good idea?" My eyes bounced off from her to Destiny, to the girl, to Mr. Spike, and back to Leslie. They were bouncing around like someone hitting a tennis ball to another opponent. "I'll go up to him anyway." I skipped my way to Mr. Spike. "Hello Mr. Spike, How you feeling? I like what you did with your hair." I said politely. Mr. Spike jerked his head at me. "Oh, it's you. I'm fine." "Why are you grumpy?" I asked. Before he could answer Leslie and Destiny both pulled me away.

We were now back at my house. "What was that all about?" And of course no one answers my demand. "Well would you look at the time we better get going." Leslie said and squirmed away towards the door. "Yeah, so bye!" Destiny screamed nervously, anxious to leave. "Why now?" I asked with a cool tone. "Silly willy we got school in the morning" Destiny said. "Yeah, so bye!" Leslie loudly said. I was finally alone and I was getting mad that Destiny and Leslie were hiding something from me. I sat down at the table, while staring at the dark sky out the window. What I couldn't get is the fact that us three were like the golden trio. I didn't expect either of them to be hiding something major from me especially as we got older and became closer. I got up and commenced to my room. Entering the room was like walking into a step in freezer. There goes the chill down my spine again. Looking around, there was nothing really much to do. I laid my clothes out for tomorrow, headed to bed, lied down, and the next thing I knew, it was already time to open my eyes for the day.

The New Kid

It's time for school and I'm still mad about yesterday. I mean what could Leslie and Destiny possibly bc hiding? I went into the kitchen and grabbed a granola bar besides that, I also reached into the refrigerator for usual wild cherry coke and headed out the door.

I started walking to school and everything was kind of weird. It was very cold outside, so I'm freezing because I'm only wearing a light, fall jacket. All of a sudden something hit me in the head. "Ow!" I said out loud. My head started bleeding. As a result I put my hand up to my head to see how much blood was there. When I took my hand and brought it back down to my view there was blood on every inch of my hand.

I looked around to see what struck me in the head. Isn't this just hilarious? All the bad things get to happen to me. On the right side of me on the ground, there was a metal object. Wow that's weird. I picked it up from the ground. It wasn't even that heavy. I looked up from the metal object to see if anyone was watching me. As I searched, no one was around so I looked back down.

All of a sudden someone pushed me and I fell onto the concrete surface. Again? really? Weren't a couple of injuries enough? Do I really need more pain? My face started burning. "Who did that?" I said attempting to get up. No one answered me. "Hello?" I said, annoyed. There was severe puffing behind me. I was still on the ground when someone kicked me and took the metal object with them. Finally I got up what felt like ten minutes later and went into my bag for a mini mirror. When I grabbed the mirror I looked into it and found that I had a scratch on the side of my forehead.

Everyone was quiet when they saw me enter the room. "What's that on your face?" Some kid asked. Mumbles of gossip were going around the room, not just because of my beaten up self, but because it's school in general. It's just the average teenage thing to do. "Nothing." I said exasperated. "But it looks like something." "Can you leave me alone?" I said getting mad. "But . . ." "I said leave me alone." My voice got kind of loud while I gritted my teeth. The kid didn't say anything, she just turned away to face her other friends.

I saw Destiny looking at my face. "Are you ok?" she asked in a startled tone, knowing that I was cranky at the second. I just ignored her. Taking notice, she had looked down at her desk in sadness because I was giving her the cold shoulder. I was still mad about last night with her and Leslie talking amongst them. Motivated by God knows what, She tried getting my attention but still I ignored her and gave her a look of annoyance. Destiny got nervous this time and looked away. Class was about to start, and I got bored so I looked around at everybody to see them all in their own little worlds. Destiny was finishing up what looked like a couple of sentences for her English homework; meanwhile the kid next to her, Clark, asked everybody for the History take home quiz answers.

"Okay students we have a new student in our class today." Mrs. Meakley's the most boring teacher ever! The kid walked in and all the girls looked like they were about to drool. "Hi sweetie, what's your name?" said Mrs. Meakley. "Oh uh it's Ja . . . Jake yea my name's Jake" the new kid acted like he wasn't too sure what his name was. Sasha, perhaps the popular girl in our grade, crossed her fingers that Jake would sit next to her. "Ok Jake you can go sit next to Vanessa." Sasha gave me a look filled with hatred. As Jake was walking to the seat next to me, he gave me a mean look. I was just looking at him like, what's your problem dude? I mean honestly, I don't even know this kid and he gave me a weird look. As I sighed, I realized that I had a whole bunch of weird things happen to me. This one is minor compared to the others. Taking a last look at him, I began to write down tonight's homework.

Creepy

Mrs. Meakley continued talking. "Class, today we're doing a textbook research instead of a lab. So I'm going to put you guys in groups of two." Oh this should be fun, I thought sarcastically to myself. "Jake, you and Vanessa will be . . ." "Can I go to the bathroom?" Jake impatiently interrupted. "Sure, take the pass." Mrs. Meakley eye bulled him suspiciously. As Jake walked, all the girls muttered. "Aw he interrupt's teacher's and he smells good, aw!" mhm, ok yea so lovely! Sasha was saying how she'd die if he asked her to senior prom. Another girl, Lily, said that he's the type of guy her mother would approve. I was thinking that all of these girls are nitwits. I mean, what do they possibly see in him? Once there is a new boy, the whole female population in our grade starts to fantasize the unknown.

I looked over to Destiny to see what she was doing. Her light brown hair was covering her face and her head was down. Could she be tired? "Destiny, lift up your head" Mrs. Meakley angrily said. Slowly,

Destiny lifted her head. She got up and started walking toward Mrs. Meakley. She looked so possessed right now. The teacher looked scared; Destiny turned to face the whole class. Eyes as red as an apple glaring at everyone, especially me. It looked like if you looked closely at her eyes, they would be like a fire becoming larger and larger.

In a blink, Destiny was on the floor. Everybody was just watching her breathe real heavy. Then she started bleeding from her arm but not too much, and her heart started to beat so loud that if you were in a different country you would be able hear it.

Jake then walked back in, he just stared at Destiny. "Someone call 911!" screamed one of the kids. People started taking out cell phones and so did Mrs. Meakley, but no one had any service which was weird. "There's always service in this class! I should know!" screamed Emma, who was sitting next to Lily. "Yes, very well, we shall discuss the cell phone usage later, Ms. Hopkins." said Mrs. Meakley, in a panicked yet annoyed voice. Jake began to walk up to Destiny; he put his hand on her shoulder. The blood from her arm started disappearing and her breathing and heartbeat were back to normal. She got up and he took his hand away from her shoulder. "I'm fine." She stated. Then her eyes went from red back to her normal baby blue eyes. As she got up I found that she, Jake, and I all were stared at each other out of nowhere. With a blink of an eye Jake disappeared and the bell rang.

Bloody

All in the hallways you could hear, "Did you see what Jake did? He must be an angel or something!" As I took a turn to my locker, Sasha was twirling her hair and obviously blabbering on and on about the so called 'wonderful, hot, sexy, new guy' that calls himself Jake. The way he fixed Destiny without even calling 911 is like a miracle brought from God." Sasha blushed, "By the way, Lily, Emma, Amy—do you guys think I have a shot with him?" "Are you kidding? How could he not miss your blonde, luxurious silky smooth hair?" complimented Lily. Amy cut in with a, "Sasha, you are the prettiest and my best friend ever, go for it girl." Sasha must have been aware with me eavesdropping on their conversation. Crunching her bag of nuts in her hands, she marched up to me leaving the others behind. Sasha gave me a look that explained hatred all over her face. "So, how's it like having the high school cutie sit next you? And let's not forget he's your partner, too." Clearly she had jealously written all over her face. I sighed, "Well, from my understanding, he went to the bathroom, we had no time to talk at all." I emphasized bathroom 'cause without a doubt I think she needed to come back to earth. "I'm not one of Jake's fan girls unlike you and your posse so it's not like I'm going to steal him away from you or anything. Do you get that? Whatever you call your jealousy should really stop; ever considered taking chill pills?" After that statement, I waved her off with a good-bye, turned on my heel and flipped my hair in her face. "Could you believe that little snot? No wonder no one likes her." Sasha infuriated as Amy, Emma, and Lily rushed up to her. What she said hurt me. Am I really unlikeable? No. that can't be true . . .

Today felt so long, it was finally time to go home. "Be careful, Vanessa." Destiny said to me as I started walking out the door of the school. "What do you mean be careful?" I questioned. "Just be careful." Destiny repeated warning me. Thoughts ran through my mind when she walked away. What does she mean by be careful? As I walked home that thought kept re-entering my mind. Today was a beyond weird day at school. I was still concerned as to why Jake seems annoyed at me without knowing me at all. Or does he?

I finally arrived at my house and noticed something different. The door was unlocked, but I was so sure that I locked it before I left. Never ever have I left my house with the doors unlocked. Literally it was impossible, I always double, even triple check the doors before leaving. Also while peering into the inside of the house; there was a hand print on the window. Whoevers hand print that smeared onto the window must have been a tiny child from the looks of it. Scared to go in, I cautiously opened the door and stepped in steadily. The door creaked as I walked in, it was quiet at first, but then a loud boom came from upstairs. I rushed to the stairs as quiet as possible. There was blood on almost all the steps. My heart was beating fast, I could barely breathe. The steps were creaking as I walked around the blood on the steps . . . This was the same nauseating blood I encountered before.

When I reached the top something really awkward happened. Out of nowhere a sharp object went and scratched the back of my neck and it slammed into the wall and fell on the floor. "Ow! This bites. Why am I so accursed?" I whispered to myself. The back of my neck was stinging like crazy. I felt like I was about to cry, the pain made me cringe. Then I heard something talk to me. "Vanessa?" I came closer to the bedroom door. "Vanessa, is that you?" Gently I grabbed the door knob turned it and walked in.

I Don't Know You

No one was in here, which was extremely weird. "Hello? This is Vanessa" I waited for an answer. All there was, was the breathing of my own self. I proceeded with precaution into the room. In the corner of my eye I saw something. It was a black object, similar to a figure. The figure shut the door and in a flash, ran across the room to the dresser.

I couldn't see the face of the dark object because it was facing its back towards me. Then it tried to talk to me; "You're Vanessa." it stated. I hesitated for a moment. "How do you know my name?" The figure started backing up. "You know me, very well my dear" Taking a deep breathe, I said, "I don't know you. Please do tell me who you are?" "Yes, you surely do. I don't need to tell you who I am. You're smart enough to presume for yourself who you could be talking to right now." the figure came closer to me. I went to say something else, but it kept talking; I was surely in a startled state of mind. "What's that?" I was just staring at the figure because it was facing its back to me and I didn't know what it was talking about. "What—what are you asking 'what's that' about?" "The thing on your neck? Scratch, is It." it sounded impatient, while questioning me fiercely. "Oh, yeah I got sliced from some sharp object, but it's not bleeding or anything." "Oh, very well, so I see." the figure said.

I took a step back away from the dark figure, wondering why I previously acted calm when I knew I was for sure not. "Don't move" it said harshly, almost like a harsh command. "You know that kid Jake, in your history class? He's the new kid?" This was so weird, how does this figure know everything? Every single diminutive detail? "How do you know he's in my history class?" "I told you Vanessa, you know me!" its voice got louder and agitated. "No!" I exclaimed, "I don't know any black figures! Get that through your brain!" I could tell the figure was getting mad by its voice and the way it started shaking.

Then, it grabbed my arm with its hand without facing me. "Listen!" just watching the figure without saying a word I listened. "You need to start talking to Jake, we're here to help you." I was very confused. "What do you mean help?" "Just listen to me Vanessa, talk to him ok? talk to him. Even if it may come off as he hates you, still do it. It's for your own sake." Finally, the figure let go of my arm. There were nail and scratch marks on my skin. "Remember, you know me. Don't take that for granted." The figure said as it went through the wall.

Why does this figure want me to talk to Jake as soon as possible? That was really creepy. The figure also said I know it. Umm c'mon, I was talking to a black figure. I haven't come across those on my long journey of pain. While I was all confused, I wondered if I still had the knife in the sink where I left it. Racing downstairs skipping over the nauseating blood, i noticed a piece of paper on the kitchen floor. So I went over and picked it up. "What's this?" I asked myself. I started reading it. A boy named Jason died a couple of years ago from . . . Jason's name now is Jake he is undercover to help . . . sincerely M.C'"

Clueless, I stood staring at the note. Jason? Jake? That's when I began to think about when I was inside the mirror. Also I began to wonder about Jake. Was he really who he said he was? What if he really is here to help? And I don't see the knife anymore which means someone really doesn't want me to have grip of the knife. But here's the question—who? Confused and agitated with other several emotions, as usual; I went to my bedroom to get some rest. I even took a shower to relax a bit and get my mind off of things that happened today. As I brushed my hair, my reflection of the mirror scared me. I don't look different, but I feel like it. It's like a warning for when a tornado is going to hit but you don't know the exact time it will arrive; disastrous. Yep. That's how I felt; like an unexpected tornado ready to do damage. Why though? I didn't have anything to be guilty for . . .

Lies

In history I attempted to talk to Jake, but everyone kept talking to him. Little Miss Sasha had to go over and flirt with him. No surprise there. "Jake, I'm very sad . . . you should comfort me with your muscular arms." She batted her eyes afterwards. Jake moved the hair out of his eyes with his hand and said, "I do go to the gym a lot." Sasha was smiling like she was about to explode. Lily patted Sasha's shoulder her giving her the 'you done good my friend' pat. Emma, on the other hand, texted away, most likely about Jake because I believe I caught her taking a pic or two of him. I was remembering Destiny cautioning me to be careful. Could she have something to do with the piece of paper? No, it couldn't. Who knows, actually?

Destiny then walked in, we both stared at each other. Jake came and was staring at me and Destiny too. "We need to talk." I told Destiny. She just looked at me. "What are you doing after school?" Destiny began to aggrandize, "uh, I'm busy." "Oh, well since you're busy today

I'll just tell you another day." I said with annoyance, trying to keep my cool. Destiny just shook her head.

Mrs. Meakley then walked in. "Morning, class." "Morning Mrs. Meakley" everyone said. "Alright today we're . . ." She stopped. Her mouth dropped open and she covered her ears. The chalk was floating in mid air and started writing. Mrs. Meakley turned to see what it was writing. "Looks like it's for Vanessa, Destiny, and Jake. All three of us, I, Jake, and Destiny stared at each other. The message on the board said "Revenge is almost here Vanessa, Destiny, and Jake, you better be careful on what you say mwahahhhahaha." Then the bell rang.

I tried catching up to Jake at lunch. "Jake?" I called out while putting my science worksheets in my book bag. "What?" he seemed annoyed, as he was avoiding eye contact with me. "You have some explaining to do" I said. "What are you talking about?" Jake said as he sat there poking at his sandwich. I reached into my bag and pulled out the piece of paper. "What is it?" asked Jake. "Oh, I don't know,"Jake", if that is your real name!" I said a bit loudly, but not too loud that everyone in the cafeteria could hear. Jake was just sitting there staring at me. He then took the piece of paper from me and started reading it. Slowly, he put the paper down with no expression on his face. "This is simply a scam, to be exact. My name is Jake, not that Jason kid. I'm alive, not dead." This Jake dude was making me suspicious. When he was done talking, he had put a smirk on his face. I eyed him, annoyed. Heck, why did he do that for? "So what you're saying is, your name is really Jake, and this note isn't fake?" We all live in a world with gummy bears and everybody is happy!" I said very curiously with a fake smile on my face. Jake stood up and placed his hand on my shoulder. "Yes, I'm positive. No need to fret. You got nothing to worry about." He still had that smirk on his face. "Lies" I whispered. "What?" "I said, lies" I repeated. "I'm not lying Vanessa." Jake laughed while shrugging his shoulders. "I'll see you later. I have to hand in my extra credit lab to

Sweeney today before the end of the day; can't afford to miss such an opportunity!" Jake picked up his lunch, threw it away, and starting walking away from me. There is something about this kid that I now fully understood. You could never be mad at him; he has his way of making others believe something.

What's that ugly thing on his neck? It was a red circle with a date inside it. The date was very hard to see from my distance. I tried squinting my eyes but I still couldn't see the date. Finally Jake was out of my site. Surely wasn't a tattoo, so what could it be? Right then the windows in the cafeteria kept opening and closing. That's when I saw the black figure facing me with its back again.

Follow

So many things happened today with me at school. As if that's any surprise. Literally, it was like everyone likes to not tell me in detail about anything. While being frustrated, I was thinking about the dark figure, Jake, and how Destiny said she had plans today. Usually she never blows me off. I remembered once when she had a doctor's appointment, but she didn't fail to walk all the way over to my house in the winter time to comfort me when I got into a fight with my mom accompanied by a stomach ache as well.

As I was walking, I saw a path. It was gray and smooth. Sort of what the clouds looked like. The path was very bright too. I wanted to see what was down that bright path, so I started walking along on the path. It was windy and cold. Indeed the path was bright, but it was also very dull in color. There was laughter, I looked around and saw nothingness among me. The laughter just kept getting louder and louder, it sounded like a witches laugh. I started running through branches of trees. While

I was doing that I heard someone behind me getting closer and closer. An opening was appearing in my sight. I quickly ran to it and lost whoever it was behind me.

When I went through the opening I found myself at a park and it wasn't bright at all. The park was called Falling Ridge Way. In this park, there was a big yellow slide that little kids were going on, some people sitting on benches smoking, and the parked smelled heavily of beer and smoke. Also, there were kids on some swings.

I started walking towards the right, when I saw Leslie and Destiny sitting and speaking on one of the benches. I went to go hide behind the park bench, because I wanted to know what they were possibly yapping about. So I listened on to their conversation. "I told Vanessa to be careful." Destiny said. "You did? What did she say?" "She looked confused and questioned me why she needed to be careful, but I didn't give her a reason; just repeated myself and I went off as quickly as possible before she ended up monitoring me." "Oh" Leslie said, "Well, are you going to tell her about the knife?" She questioned. I was getting mad now. What did they know about the knife that I didn't know about? Was it really too hard to blurt it out to me? "The knife? I don't know Leslie, because you know what the possibilities are if we tell Vanessa! They won't tally up good!" What possibilities? I thought to myself. "Yeah that's true . . . oh no. This cannot be good."

Leslie said worried. "What?" Destiny's voice was scared. "She's going to do something bad. Don't you smell the strong perfume? Kind of like pineapples." Destiny smelled the air. "Oh my God, yes! We must get out of here!" Destiny screamed ready to pounce off out of the bench. After a moment they got up. I also started getting up as well; I was tempted to follow them. But as I got up I tripped over a branch and hit my left cheek against a hard rock. Both Destiny and Leslie turned around and said, "Vanessa?" I looked them straight in the eye and got up.

The clouds started to get darker. Thunder and lightning came next, it also started raining. The next thing everyone knew, lightening stroke the big slide. A couple of kids were still on it. The screws on the slide somehow became unscrewed and the very large slide came crashing down and landed on a little seven year old girl and she was dead. The two five year old boys were on the slide severely hurt and everyone went quiet. The sight of it all was quite unbearable to see.

"What just happened back there?" I asked. They both just looked at each other and then back at me. "How much of our conversation did you hear anyway?" asked Leslie, concerned. "All of it . . ." Both of them were quiet. You could see the regret that lies within their eyes. "And I want the truth." I was silent for a moment, "Now." Leslie and Destiny just stood there still quiet. "I'm waiting! Give me the damn truth!" I said impatiently while waving my airs with abruptness. "We uh, really can't tell you." Destiny finally spoke up. "Well, why the hell not?" I said still impatiently, as my voice grew louder and firmer. "Because then me and Destiny would have to face the consequences." Leslie said frightened. "Yeah, but it's not like you guys are going to get killed by just telling me, right?" There was silence. "Right?" I said questioningly "Well, not exactly Vanessa." Destiny gulped. "What do you mean, Destiny?" "I really wish I could tell you, I really do." "Ok, well can you tell me anything about the knife?" "No." "Not even a little bit?" "No Vanessa, we're sorry." Destiny sounded like she felt bad. "Yeah, but let us tell you something." "What?" I asked Leslie. "Be careful, be very careful." Leslie and Destiny said at the same time. "I know to be careful! I'm not stupid, but would you guys stop telling me to become careful, it's irritating me. Plus, it's not like telling me to be careful is going to solve anything! You're just warning me! A warning is nothing but a warning.

and the truth is the truth! Can you hear me in those big heads of yours?"
I was annoyed.

We walked onto 23rd street. All three of us didn't talk for a while,
until we got lost. "Where are we?" Destiny questioned. "Yeah, I don't
know Destiny." I said. "I think we're in the valley." Leslie said. I looked
back to look at her. She had out her phone. I think she was texting
someone, but I don't really know. "Hey guys, lets turn this corner."
Leslie declared. So we all turned the corner just like she told us too.

It was so dark over there. No one could see anything. It made me
think of the forest Snow White went through to get to the Dwarfs
house, although this didn't seem like a happy ending or a light at the
end of the tunnel. There was only the laughter of that person who
sounded like a witch. "What's that noise?" Destiny asked, panicked.
"I don't know" I said. "Destiny? Vanessa? Is that you?" Leslie asked.
"No, I'm not that close to you" I said. "Neither am I!" said Destiny. In
a flash, we heard Leslie scream and get whacked up against the wall of
the building. Then there was crying. It came from Destiny. "Why are
you crying?" "Because Leslie is hurt, it's sad." We rushed through the
dark to find Leslie.

A building light came on and we saw Leslie, she was covered with
bruises and her mouth was open with pain. Also, the number one,
three, two popped up next to Leslie. This must be what the number
on the knife symbolized. I drew my attention away from the building
number and searched around; no sign of the person that whacked Leslie
anywhere. Destiny and I just looked at each other, worried written all
over our faces. Next thing we knew, we're smacked up against the wall
staring at something that was getting closer to us. It was the knife that
we saw. Someone then threw it at me and Destiny. The knife landed in
between us. Laughter came next. "Did you actually think I would leave
you alone?" "Where's that noise coming from?" I whispered to Destiny.

"I don't know, Vanessa. I really don't." Destiny whispered back. That's when she popped out. "You missed me sis?" "Chenelle! I thought I scared you off? "You may have killed uncle bob but that doesn't bother me." Chenelle stared at me with a big, huge smile on her round face. I tried to get away from the wall, but it seemed to be that I was stuck. "Ok, so what do you really want? Do you want money? To be famous? What? Maybe a humongous mansion with you and your future rich husband" A life of joblessness?" The big huge smile on Chenelle's face disappeared. Her expression became still and study. She came straight up to my face and said, "I want you dead and I won't rest until that happens. Don't try to act smart and sarcastic with me, you hear?"

Chenelle then took the knife and pointed it at my neck. I, on the other hand, turned to look at Destiny. She gave me a 'sorry I didn't tell you' kind of look. I just turned back around to look at Chenelle. "Hah, it's such a pity how you are. But thanks for telling me that you want me dead Chenelle because now I can be extra careful when something bad happens." I whacked the knife out of Chenelle's hand. It left a scratch across my right hand as I stricken it. "Oh, so I see you're putting your brain to work? Haha no, you see that's where you are wrong. I have someone new watching every move you make." Chenelle then backed up and ran away into the darkness.

What's next?

Leslie, Destiny, and I had found our way back to my house. Now, we were all quiet sitting on the couch glancing at each other. Eventually we all started talking. "We're really sorry we didn't tell you about Chenelle." Destiny said. "Alright, it's ok I guess. Just tell me how or where you guys saw her?" Destiny started to answer, but Leslie cut her off. "Well, it was like one or two months ago. Destiny and I were at Falling Ridge Way getting ice cream from the ice cream truck. So after that we started walking away, it turned out we found ourselves in this path with lots of bushes and trees around." Destiny took over the conversation from there. "Yeah, so as we were walking, we heard laughter, so we started walking faster. Then there was movement behind us so we ran and tripped over some vines. We then looked up and saw someone's feet. We looked up all the way and it was Chenelle. She told us to get up so we did as scared as can be. She showed us the knife and how bad she wanted you dead. Chenelle also threatened us not to tell you unless she would kill us. Then she told us to go home and keep our lips sealed, or else." "That's it?" I asked somewhat relieved. "Yes" I studied both Destiny and Leslie to see their reactions. Leslie was just playing with her phone with a little smile on her face. It must be a guy that she's interested in. Destiny, well, she looked worried and scared as if the truth was still lacking. "Ok, I'm confused." I said. "About what?" they both said. "Well you guys just told me what happened, does that mean she's going to kill the both of you?" "No, she just saw us and told you that she wanted you dead. So I doubt it." Destiny said. Leslie just laughed. "What's so funny?" I rudely questioned. "Nothings going to happen to any of us, I bet Chenelle is just threatening us. She's probably scared of you, Vanessa." Leslie seemed so confident in her answer. "So what you're saying is that what's up next is we're all going to be fine, like back to normal?" "Well not exactly Vanessa, but almost one-hundred percent normal." Leslie giggled. I just gave Leslie a look and kept talking.

"The dark figure." I said. "Dark figure?" Leslie seemed shocked. "Yeah, dark figure. You guys no anything about that?" I was curious. "No, I don't know anything about the dark figure." Destiny said. "Me neither." Leslie announced as she put away her phone. Then there was a movement, it got cold in the living room where we were. We looked around to see what that movement was.

Revealed

Next to the TV was the dark figure wearing a hood to cover its face. I came to take Vanessa on a little journey." The figure said. "What journey?" I was annoyed again. "You have to come with me to find out." "Don't go with that thing Vanessa!" Leslie shouted. I ignored her. "Why should I go with you?" I asked the figure. "Look, do you want to find out who I am or not? I promise I am good." I looked at Destiny and Leslie and said, "I'll be right back."

So the dark figure took my hand, and we went through the wall. We went through this portal, very fast. I had landed on my face smacked against the floor. "Alright, I came with you, now who are you? I need at least some type of answering up in here! I don't just go traveling with strangers for the heck of it!" I asked while crossing my arms. "Look, where we are." As I got up I looked around. That's when I saw it. It was the mirror that I saw awhile ago. "Oh my god, you know about the mirror?" I asked as I was staring at the broken mirror. "Yeah I do.

Remember who you were running away from?" "Yeah, that Jason dude." I said. "Do you know what his name is now?" asked the dark figure. "Well, I saw the paper you dropped and it said his name now is Jake, but he's really dead and his name really is Jason, but he won't admit it to me." I said. "Yeah, Jason could be a pain, stubborn he is. But does that give you a hint of who I am, Vanessa?" "No it doesn't. It just tells me that Jake is really Jason, and he's dead." "Think Vanessa, really think. I know Chenelle's your sister, she had my dad kill me. Remember?" I looked away from the mirror and faced the dark figure with fear. "You mean, Uncle Bob?" "Yeah, Uncle Bob. He's my dad." Now, I had a pretty good idea on who the dark figure was. "I think I know who you are now?" I said kind of scared because I wasn't sure. Slowly, the dark figure took down its hood. "Holy crap!" I screamed. "Yeah, it's me" "Melissa!" I was so happy I forgot almost every pain in this universe. "Wait, if you and Jason are really dead, how can you guys talk to people?" "Well, it's simple, we're spirits. Good spirits, not the ones that haunt cemeteries on Halloween." Melissa said as I giggled. "Oh okay." I smiled. "Why couldn't you had just told me before that you were my cousin Melissa?!" "Because I wanted to wait until after you saw Chenelle . . . Oh, and you can't tell anyone it's me ok? If your friends ask, say I don't know the figure wouldn't tell me . . . got it? Make anything up, just don't reveal my identity!." I looked at Melissa very carefully, "Okay, I won't. You have my word." "Well, let's get you back before Destiny and Leslie start to think I strangled you or stabbed you or whatever it is that they may think." We both laughed.

I arrived at the house with Melissa. Who was covering herself with the hood so Leslie and Destiny wouldn't know that it was her. Both Destiny and Leslie stared at us. "I'll be watching you, remember that." said Melissa. She then disappeared out of nowhere.

Discussion

Time to go to school once again, I was thinking as I woke up. Destiny and Leslie left yesterday without saying a word. It was kind of weird because we always say bye to each other, but oh well.

We were in history class now waiting for Mrs. Meakley to come in. Instead some grown man came in. "Hello class I'm your new teacher Mr. Bagu." "What!" the whole class exclaimed. "Where's Mrs. Meakley?" one of the kids asked in the back corner of the room. Mr. Bagu stared at us with tragedy. "She got killed by that serial killer that killed a lot of people a while ago." The whole class was tragic now. Mutters of suspicion were heard around the room. "Ok well, let's go to work."

As Mr. Bagu was handing out worksheets, I tried to have a discussion with Jake, which is actually Jason. "Hey. can we talk?" Jake looked up from his desk, he was scribbling his name on his notebook. "Oh, it's you again. What do you want this time?" He seemed cranky.

A tad bit more than last time we talked. "Listen." I whispered, quietly while looking around to see if anyone could hear us. "I know you lied about who you really are, Melissa told me. Please don't deny it this time." "Can we finish this conversation another time?" he said abruptly, obviously not wanting to take this conversation any further. "Fine, can we chitchat at lunch then?" I asked. "Yeah, at lunch. Sounds like it'll be a joy to sit with you again for lunch like last time" His voice came out flat and sarcastic. For the rest of the period, we were quiet. I didn't talk to him or anybody else in the room. Neither did Jason; he sat there drawing superheroes like superman, Spiderman. And he even drew Scooby-doo; Even though Scooby isn't a superhero from a comic book. When Sasha attempted flirting with Jake he didn't even acknowledge her presence. I bet I knew what she was thinking, 'Oh, Jake so digs me. But why isn't he flirting back is it my breath? I took this guess because her hand was placed on her mouth in shock of Jake's reaction towards her. Should I ask Amy to reach into her big bag and grab the mints for me?' After forty minutes of silence, the bell at last rang.

It was time to go to lunch. I went to sit across from Jason. As I began talking to him, I saw Destiny giving me a look like I should be sitting with her instead of him. Let her be mad, she truly deserves it for keeping an unbelievably huge secret from you. I was telling myself this to fill in for the guilt. I tried ignoring the daggers from Destiny and put all my concentration together and focus on Jason. "Okay, so how much did she tell you?" Jason, without hesitation, blurted out while aggressively munching on his turkey with cheese sandwich. "Everything. I knew you're real name wasn't Jake from the start but you wouldn't admit it to me." Jason looked down at his feet. "So what? I'm dead. My real name is Jason big deal!" Jason loudly whispered. "Calm down, do you want people to hear you . . . Melissa also told me that you guys were here because of Chenelle?" "She did? Oh wow. I hate Chenelle. I really do." Jason madly said. "Who would have guessed with your teeth grinding together . . . hey, I got a question for you though." I told him. "What? What could possibly be your question now?" "Why do you hate me so much?" "Why? You really want to know huh? Well, you disturbed me and Melissa when we Were inside the mirror in peace. We didn't need your butt there while thinking of a plan to save you. That's probably how Chenelle tracked you down. Oh and plus you're Chenelle's sister so I simply cannot stand your company." Jason hissed.

I took a few sips of my cool blue sports bottle Gatorade before speaking again. "So? I'm nothing like her and besides she wants to kill me and supposedly has someone watching me on every step I take. Just because you are the same blood, doesn't mean same personality traits." Jason gave me a worried face. "Aw, it sounds like she would do something like hiring someone to watch you. But don't tell anyone about this conversation we just had ok?" "Well, Ok, but before I go, I have one more question to ask you." I stated. "What is it?" "The thing on your neck, with a date inside it, what is it? I saw it the other day and I'm really curious about it." Jason lifted his head, put his hand on the back of his neck, and brought it back down to the table. He took a deep breathe and started to speak. "When I was killed, Chenelle grabbed my head and carved 2008 into my neck and made a circle around it. Then, she threw me into a wet, dark place which was where the mirror is now and I met Melissa there a year later. She had told me about Uncle Bob and how he was her father. That is pretty sad. I mean how can you kill your own daughter? That's incredibly psycho path to do!" "Wow, I wonder why Chenelle would kill you. I never even met you before, and yeah, my Uncle Bob was a pretty messed up person he didn't like my family one bit." I said. "I know, but I had almost everything I wanted and Chenelle didn't like that because I used to go out with her and she got pissed seeing everything I had. In my opinion that's no reason to kill anyone. Jeez, I wonder what she would've done over jealousy of me talking to other girls. Just the thought of that scares me." "That's so mean of her! She shouldn't have done that! Is she that insane! Really, could a person get that mad over something?" I shouted. "Yeah, but talk to you later ok? I, uh, have to go clean my eye out; I got crumbs of my sandwich crust inside it." Jason's eyes were getting red. "Ok bye. I will see you around." I waved as I walked to go sit next to Destiny.

The Scary Dream

Another productive day at school, what's new? I was getting super tired. Destiny walked home with me. "Vanessa?" I looked at Destiny, "Yeah?" "Why were you sitting with Jake at lunch?" "Um I had to tell him something that's all." I was getting nervous now. "And that would be . . . ?" asked Destiny in a mean tone. "Just something okay? Don't worry about it plus, you like to keep secrets from me so let me have one of my own." Destiny and I were quiet the rest of the way home.

Since it was a Friday night, Destiny slept over. It was already midnight and I was falling asleep. While Destiny was wide awake listening to music and on the computer checking out her face book page. I finally fell asleep to the song Every time We Touch by Cascada on my bean bag chair. That's when I had the scariest dream ever next to the dream I had months ago. This is how the not so lovely dream went.

I was on the street in the fogginess; the wind was blowing like an angry stampede taking over the world. It was crazy. Then the fog cleared up. When the fog went away I saw dead people lying down on the streets. It reminded me of that time at school with everyone lying down on the ground unable to speak. Something then sliced off my hand. My hand landed on the ground. Blood was pouring out of my wrist now. I started running out of nowhere. Someone grabbed me and threw me into this dark,mysterious place. The lights came on after a minute. A sudden force came upon my ankles. Quickly, I looked down and found that it was Zack and Andrew's dead body's at my feet. I stood there staring at them with tears in my eyes. They got up . . . Zack had a pipe in his hand, while Andrew had a piece of metal in his. And not just any old piece of metal, but the metal that thwacked me in the middle of the street. "You done this to us, Vanessa. Pay for it!" They exclaimed. "No I didn't! I swear you two mean everything to me!" "We're going to hurt you now. We promise you won't feel anything! Well, once your dead like us!" Andrew and Zack came at me and started smacking me with the pipe and metal. "Don't hurt me, please don't hurt me! I beg you! Stop it, please!" "Good-bye forever, Vanessa. We wish it didn't have to end like this, but what can you do about it?" Andrew and Zack said as they went for the top of my head. I started screaming even more at the top of my lungs.

"Don't hurt me! Zack, Andrew, Please don't!" I screeched. "Vanessa, Vanessa!" "I said don't hurt me!" "Vanessa wake up!" "Ah!" I screamed and woke up. "I'm alive!" I happily screamed. Destiny just stared at me and said. "Why yes you are alive." I started to touch my heart, shoulders, arms. Legs, and especially my hand. "Ok, good I'm breathing. I'm still here. Oh my god!" "What?" asked Destiny. "I have a hand!" "Really? I had no idea, so do I. Did you also know I also have a nose?" Destiny sarcastically said. I then got up, aggressively put my hands on Destiny's shoulder and started shaking her. "I love you girl!" Destiny looked at me in a weird way and took my hands off her shoulder. "Hey Vanessa I got a very important question for you." "Huh? What would that be ?" I was all smiley. "Are you high?" My smiling face went away. I looked Destiny straight in the eye and started cracking up. It turned out I spit on her because she put on a face and wiped it away with her hand. "Nah. I'm not high, I just had a scary dream, that's all." I was smiling again. "Did you really?" Destiny asked with disbelief. "I'm serious Destiny! Look at my wrist!" I showed her my wrist that had a scar around it. "Wow, Vanessa." Destiny touched my scar. "Ow! Don't touch it, it hurts." my smile went away. "Sorry. I didn't know it would hurt." said Destiny said, apologetically. We both looked up and started laughing.

Gone

It's Saturday morning now and Leslie just came over. She walked through the front door and into the kitchen where Destiny and I sat on the stools. "Good morning, people." Leslie said. "Morning!" I shouted. "Yeah, morning." Destiny sounded exhausted as she yawned. "You guys want to try this new drink I got from the Food and Beverage store?" Leslie asked. "Nah." Destiny said. "Oh I want to try!" I claimed. "Of course she does." Destiny was cranky. Leslie had on a bright smile. "Perfect, here you go" and handed it to me. "Yum, this stuff is good!" I yelled.

After a while I started uncontrollably laughing. "Leslie, what was in that drink you gave Vanessa?" "Oh, I don't know let me see." Leslie picked up the bottle she gave me. Meanwhile I'm laughing my butt off on the couch. Leslie was taking forever so Destiny's like, "That's it give me the bottle!" "ahahahaha you guys are fighting over a bottle! Get it? Bottle! Woo! I'm too funny!" I announced and screamed while I was rolling on the floor laughing. Destiny and Leslie looked at me for a second and then went back to talking to each other. "Okay then, anyway let's see the ingredients, red 20, blue 5, caffeine, juice, and laughing gas. Laughing gas! You see there's our problem right there! Don't you read anything before buying! What if it was a poisonous container?" Destiny yelled to Leslie. Leslie was too busy texting. "Who in the world are you texting? Does it really look like the time to be doing that?" Destiny asked Leslie. "No one important, just relax." Leslie smiled. I was still laughing, but I finally got up. "So what are you guys doing here? Do you live here?" I laughed like a maniac. Leslie and Destiny looked at me. "You invited us." said Leslie. "Oh! Ha-ha that's a knee slapper right there! I said out loud and slapped my knee.

It was now eleven at night and I was still laughing. There was a storm outside, it was raining very hard, there was lightening, and thunder which was really loud. The electricity then went out and Destiny went to get a flashlight and turned it on. A loud thump and the shattering of glass went all over the floor. It came from the back door. Everyone was quiet except for me, of course. "What's going on?" Destiny asked with fear. "I don't know! Maybe the sky is dancing?" I shouted with fear. "Ok thank you, Vanessa for the insight!" Destiny shouted back. That's when she came in. "It worked?" asked Chenelle. "Yeah. Let me tell you it was very easy indeed to get her to drink it." said Leslie. "Oh my god! Wait Leslie you're on her side? Since when did this happen?" "Shut up!" Chenelle yelled at Destiny. "Leslie here's the gun take Vanessa up to her room and shoot her." "What!" Destiny screamed. "I'm going to lock this one up in the bathroom and then I'll be right up with you." "Ok" Leslie and Chenelle laughed. Chenelle grabbed Destiny's arm and said, "Lets go, shrimp. You're wasting my time." Leslie grabbed my arm and pulled me up the stairs, as Destiny was screaming my name.

Leslie and I were now in my room alone. She put me down on the chair. I just kept laughing away at everything. She held the gun up to me and took a deep breath while cocking it. Suddenly I stopped laughing and became serious. "Oh crap. The laughing gas wore off . . ." Leslie nervously said. I turned to look at Leslie. I saw her because the window shade was up overshadowing the sight of the moon and there was lightening still. "What are you doing?" I curiously asked. "Me? Oh nothing. Just relax." "Well then why is there a gun in your hand?" Leslie took her hand and put it on my mouth. "Just hear me out, I'm going to shoot you and you're not going to feel anything because it'll be over in three seconds, instantaneous death!" I smacked her arm so she would get her hand off my mouth. "I thought you were on my side?" I asked. "Well, you thought incorrect, Ms. Knowledge. You think you know everything that's going on around you when you really don't. I've been the one watching you all these years. I was never on your side because you are a selfish prick, and who forgets about their sister as if they were nothing?" Leslie went to pull the trigger. The door opened and slammed shut and pushed Leslie which made her pull the trigger even quicker. The bullet went through my arm. I cringed in pain.

There was the sound of a wrench hitting against Leslie. "Hello?" I asked to see who it was. "It's me, Destiny." Her voice shook more than ever. There was blood all over her from killing Leslie with a wrench. "I thought you were locked up in the bathroom?" "You heard that?" "Yeah, I might have been acting weird but I listened." I said. "Hah, well Chenelle forgot to lock the door." We both laughed and smiled. "Speaking of Chenelle . . . where is she?" Destiny and I both stared at each other and our smiles disappeared. "Let's get out of my room." I whispered, with fear. So we exited my room and went into the hall where it was pitch black. "Vanessa, can I tell you something?" "Sure, what?" "Ok, if anything happens please don't forget me." I slowed down and grabbed Destiny's hand to make sure she was still behind me. "Listen up Destiny, I'm not going to forget you, you are the closest thing I got and I want you to know that ok?" I started tearing.

I got no response back. I realized that I was no longer holding Destiny's hand anymore. "Are you flipping kidding me, crap!" I shouted out into the darkness. I searched the whole house for Destiny, but there was nothing but silence. This would have been a heck of a lot easier if had that flashlight Destiny was holding with me. Instead, I had to feel my way around the house. Until, I heard Destiny screaming. It was coming from the basement, so I ran down there as fast as I could. I saw Chenelle start to pull the trigger while Destiny was up against the wall with a rope around her neck. It was tight but not tight enough to choke her to death. When Chenelle started pulling the trigger I shouted, "No!" Chenelle was laughing with evilness. Destiny said, "Bye . . . Forever." she shredded a tear. "No!" I shouted again. Chenelle shot Destiny three times, once in the heart, and twice in the head. Blood splattered all over the both of us.

Just standing, looking at the stream of blood coming to my feet, Destiny was now gone. "Well, well, well, how sad. The poor baby lost the battle. Now didn't I always tell you that I will always win? Never underestimate me." Chenelle chuckled then turned to me. "Now, it's your turn to die and I'll be satisfied with my life. Everyone will come to me for their problems instead of you, the one who gets everything they ever wanted. Oh, how you remind me of Jason." "I don't think so! I will not let you ruin my life! Maybe people come to me instead of you is because I don't kill people once they piss me off!" I yelled with tears running down my face and my voice all scratchy. On the floor, there was a big rock. I took it, picked it up, and threw it at the gun. She dropped it and made it fly across the room. We both went for it. Chenelle pushed me on the floor and now was on top of me. I smacked her across the face and she grabbed my neck. She started choking me. The gun was in the reach of me so I grabbed it and kicked Chenelle off from me. I cleared my throat and said, "This is it." I said, "Your time is up. No more of your crap. I can finally live satisfied!" Chenelle just looked at me with no sense of care what's so ever. I aimed the gun and pulled the trigger a couple of times in her heart. When I was done I threw the gun on the floor. I went directly up to her, "That's what you get for messing with me and our family. The knife appeared to be right next to her. So I picked it up and grabbed Chenelle forcefully and I carved 2010 in the back of her neck and circled it. Revenge is sweet.

I had thrown Chenelle's body into the lake, leaving her there to drown. Back at my house, was a big bloody mess. I ended up cleaning for hours until it was spotless. When I finished cleaning, it looked as if nothing happened. Which was good, of course.

Jason and Melissa entered through the front door on a Wednesday night. "Hey Vanessa. We saw you throw Chenelle's body into the lake." Melissa said. "Oh you did? Wow. Yup I had to do it. I had to get rid of the evidence." I answered back. Jason came up to me. "For one thing I am beyond proud of you, you gave that jerk a piece of her own medicine!" Jason hugged me as if it was the happiest day of his life, "We're Glad to know everything's all good now; but, Melissa and I must go now." I paused from what Jason said. I didn't want them to leave, I wanted them to stay with me. "what do you mean you guys must go? Guys, you're the only two I have now. Nobody else is going to be as close anymore, especially with Destiny gone. She was one of the very things that were very close to me and I lost her. Don't make me lose you guys forever as well. I grew a hate for that word." Melissa and Jason glanced at each other and then came to sit next to me. "Our times up, we came to help you but now our work here is done. We only came to help you, Vanessa. We gave you hints to Chenelle and made you a stronger person. We wish we could stay, but unfortunately it doesn't work out that way." I nodded, still refusing to accept this on the inside. They both got up and headed toward the door. I just stared at them without saying anything, sadness was what I felt. "Oh and Vanessa, be safe and careful. You don't want to find yourself dead, like Destiny." Jason announced. "You're right Jason, there's a store right round the block that sells knives like machetes, don't need anybody buying it for me, you know?" Melissa, Jason, and I all laughed and then they disappeared through the door.

There you have it, my story. Chenelle used to be a sweetheart, but I don't know why she left. I never meant to break her soul and make her turn evil. I guess I should have shown more care and affection towards her. On my to do list is, to be nicer to people. I may even say sorry to Germy Godzilla—I mean Gregory too tomorrow for being such a heartless bully.

I am now alone. It is ten at night, and very dark outside. I went to the living room to watch TV because that's the only thing a lonely person like me could do. When I pressed the on button on the remote there was shocking news. "Oh my gosh." I said out loud. I really cannot believe it. The people were talking about Chenelle's body that was thrown into the lake. How the heck did they know about that? Is there some kind of hidden security camera there that I should have known about before doing my dirty business?

"This is news at night; do you know where your children are? Well we got some breaking news for all you folks out there. A girl's body was found in a lake called 'Lake Washington' not too long ago. The cops are going door to door asking people if they know this girl. If you do be honest with us. We want to serve our country well and do the poor girl justice in finding her murderer!" "Umm Jenny? Slight problem . . ." "Yeah, Mr. Kyle?" "it appears to be that Her body's missing" "We'll be right back, Washington!"

A commercial came on. Meanwhile I got a knock on the door. It must be the cops. "Hi. May we have a word with you?" "Okay, you may." I tried to say without coming off as nervous. "Do you know this girl by any chance?" One of the police men showed me Chenelle's picture. "Uh no actually, I don't, sorry I can't help you." "It's okay ma'am, thanks for your concern and time." After they left I sat back down, worried. Chenelle's body's missing that could only mean one thing right? The lights went out and the TV started flashing black and white. A loud thump hit against the window, and I went up to it. Terrified, I pushed away the curtains . . . Chenelle's dead body came through the window. She lifted my head back with one finger making me fall backward onto the floor. She jumped on top of me, and grabbed out a knife. "I always win, Vanessa pay back is what I call it. Go ahead and be sorry for the life you led, for your mistakes, but you know what? No one is going to care once you're gone. Want to know why? It's simple; all of the people that care about you are now dead. So, in a way I'm helping you to be happy; I'm relieving what you call stress, isn't that a plus?" She pointed the knife directly to my heart. I started screaming, "NO!" "Any last words, sis?" I thought of something to say real fast. "This isn't real, it's all a dream. Am I right? You can't kill me! It's a dream! All of it! Can't you get over my flaws and begin a new life with me to try making things right between us? Oh wait, that's impossible because you're dead!" "Maybe it is all a dream or maybe you're just hallucinating! Either way it doesn't matter! Have you ever heard of a scary dream leading to a person really dying in their sleep? I'm going to kill you now!" "WAIT, please stop! And think of all the old times we had together before you disappeared from my life! Like that guy you liked!" Chenelle still held the same position she has been in this whole time with her voice even more angry than before. "Oh, like for example Zack? The one who liked you? The one that you liked back? Is this supposed to make me feel better? No matter what you do or say I will finish you!" "Okay, maybe that was a bad thing to bring up, but what about Christmas time! Mom and Dad gave you one-hundred dollars and me nothing!" "Vanessa Rose Martinez you're piggy bank was over flowing with money! You don't deserve any more money than you already had! The least you could have done was realize that I wasn't there anymore to help you ask out guys or flirt with them! You couldn't even go looking for me! I hear you saying that you will become a better person, but I do not believe a word that comes out of your mouth. After I stick this knife through your heart, never again will you mess with me." I quickly said another thing stalling her. "I know a dream can kill you, but I lived through two tough dreams, and I'm still here! So go ahead stab me Chenelle! This isn't so!" I shouted at her. "You're not going to open eyes tomorrow morning and think things are fine, 'cause they won't be. Eyes are very fragile, Vanessa. Once your dead they can either be opened or closed, and I choose closed for you. You know, so no one sees those ugly eyes of yours!" There's nothing left I can do. Chenelle won't budge. I tried everything but didn't succeed. And I realize, if this was a dream, I would be awake by now. The rain came into the living room making clicking sounds. As I can say good-bye to my life. Chenelle raised the knife and with her zombie-like face grinning wide, she stabbed me right through the heart.